Open House

By: TC Matson

Love,
TC Matson

Cover Design by: © Sara Eirew Photography
Editing by: Amanda Brown

ISBN-13: 978-1542612159
ISBN-10: 1542612152

Dedication

The sun always shines behind the storm clouds. The night always gives
way to the day.

Stay Strong.

Chapter 1

Love. The dictionary says it's an intense feeling of deep affection—to feel a deep romantic or sexual attachment to someone.

When you meet your special someone, the one you know you'll marry, deep in your soul, the one you love so immensely, you see yourself growing old and gray, dancing with each other in walkers at the same nursing home until you're no longer a body in this world. You swear your love to them—"To have and to hold, for better or for worse, for richer or for poorer, in sickness and in health, to love and to cherish from this day forward until death do us part."

I've dreamed of the day I could say those very words to my long, *very* longtime boyfriend, Brian. I've fantasized about what it would be like to walk down the aisle in a white flowing dress toward him in a tux as he grinned proudly and from ear to ear. You'd think after eleven years of dating we would have already taken that step. Nope. Brian doesn't care for marriage. In fact, his very words were, "I don't need someone to tell me I have a wife." He's fallen short on the understanding of how marriages work.

But we have said our vows. We were in bed. I was pregnant. And he loved me.

I've stuck true to our fake little vows over the course of our time together. But no one ever told me that at times the "for worse" can be so decayed that you live your life as a robot. You become complacent. Unhappy. You walk the same steps daily, basically becoming a routine, day in and day out. Sometimes I wonder what would happen if I opened a different cabinet drawer instead of the usual one. Would the pull of the universe shift and the whole world collapse?

I'd be lying if I told you I haven't tried just to see what happens. Luckily for my son and me, the universe didn't implode. Actually, it was very anticlimactic. The only thing that happened—the drawer opened. Big surprise.

That's where I am. Staring at the kitchen drawers, waiting for the coffee to finish, and wondering if this time when I grab a spoon, something will shift in my day.

The coffee maker gurgles and bubbles the last few seconds of its brew. I watch as the dark liquid falls into the pot, creating ripples to spread, and wakes to splash into the glass. The house creaks above me where I know Brian has just gotten out of the shower. Regardless if it was the last thing he did before going to sleep, he requires one every morning. "It wakes me up," he has told me for the past decade.

I grab my white coffee cup that says "Mom Rocks" on it as well as his travel mug and fill them both to the top. I don't dare add creamer and sugar to his as I do mine. He desires his one way and one way only, regardless of how many times I've tried convincing him my way adds a sweet and powerful kick. He insists his bitter jolt is much stronger and wakes him up faster, giving him the extra oomph for the day.

I grab the toaster from the corner of the counter, slide two pieces of bread into the slots, and push the button down. As it toasts, I pause for a moment to enjoy the sweet aroma of my coffee before taking a sip and then getting the butter.

Regardless of how many times I've done this, whether I'm watching it or not, when the bread pops up, it always scares the living shit out of me. Today is no different, except that it's brought an ounce of laughter into my morning routine.

"What are you laughing about?" Brian asks rounding the corner into the kitchen.

"The terrorizing toaster." I point to the evil thing with the butter knife.

His left brow raises as he studies me like I've lost my damn mind, but the amused expression quickly slips away. "My coffee ready?" he asks nodding toward his travel mug.

My smile dissipates. "Yes. Would you like toast this morning?"

"Yeah," he hollers over his shoulder heading into the living room to gather his things for work.

"Do you have a busy day today?" I wrap his toast in a paper towel.

He tucks his grimy white hard hat under his arm. "Not too bad. Why?"

I shrug. "Just asking."

He offers a lopsided smile, one I know isn't filled with any emotion. "I'll come home early and we'll spend some time together."

I give the best smile I can conjure up. I've heard the same line for years now. Early never comes. Neither does us spending time together. In his eyes, my demand for "us time" should be sufficed by him in the recliner and me on the couch because, technically speaking, we're in the same room thus spending much-needed time together.

He reaches around my shoulder, grabs the toast, and kisses me on the cheek. "I'll see you later."

The scent of his cologne—spicy and musky—lingers for much longer than he was around and I take a long inhale, relishing the scent.

I bought that cologne for him many years ago for our anniversary, just knowing he'd enjoy it. I was strolling through the mall one day and a bright red bottle, centered in the glass showcase, caught my eye. All I was going to do was take a look at the fancy little bottle, but when the older lady with white hair sprayed it on the tester card, I knew right then and there I wasn't walking away without it. I placed it in a small blue bag with green polka-dots, shoved some white tissue around it, and later that evening, I gave it to him. At first I could tell he wasn't that into it, but that was before he got a sniff of the amazing scent. He grinned so big afterward and immediately sprayed a little on him. There was something about that cologne that made me unable to keep my hands off him. We both enjoyed that night. And even after years of buying the same bottle, it still has the same effect on me.

"Dad just leave?" The raspy, just-woke-up, voice of Lucas fills my ears.

I twirl around. "Good morning, sweetie. You're up really early."

He nuzzles against me, hugging me. "I forgot to close my curtains last night."

"Shut them and go back to sleep," I tell him.

He shakes his head. "Already tried."

"Did you at least sleep well?" I place a kiss on top of his head.

"Yeah." He lets loose and heads straight for the refrigerator.

Ever since he was a baby, when he woke up, he wanted something to eat. And now that he's ten, nothing has changed, except he isn't in a crib fussing for food. Now, he's old enough to roll right out of bed and get something himself, but the demand is just the same.

"Can you make pancakes?" he asks with innocent and hopeful eyes.

"Somehow I knew you were going to want some today, so I made a few last night. Grab them out of the freezer and I'll warm them up."

His hazel eyes widen with happiness. He spins around and jerks open the freezer door, reaches in and grabs the bag. I warm two of them up for him as he grabs some orange juice and jumps onto the stool at the island.

"When is open house? Today or tomorrow?" he asks.

"It's tomorrow," I reply.

He nods. "I thought so, just wasn't sure. I really hope I get Mrs. Sheets."

"And why's that?" I ask placing the pancakes in front of him.

"She's really nice. Coby had her last year and said she was super laid back. Not strict at all. And she likes watching movies."

"I'm sure whoever you have will be great."

He shakes his head. "Not if I get Mrs. Dalton." He shakes his body, overemphasizing a shudder. "I've heard she can silence you with one look. And if you drop your pencil, you'll have silent lunch."

I laugh, leaning down on my elbow. "She sounds super mean."

He looks at me with the most serious expression. "She's really mean. Homework for hours, mean."

I gasp facetiously. "Homework for hours?"

"Seriously, Mom. If I get her, please remember me."

I burst out laughing. "I'm sure she isn't *that* bad."

"You have no clue!" he exclaims. "She's a witch."

"Lucas. Watch your words. That wasn't very nice."

He drops his fork. "When she puts a spell on me you'll see."

There isn't any use in arguing with a head-strong ten-year-old, so I leave the conversation alone and grab my coffee before checking my phone. Sometimes Brian will be sweet and text me when he gets to work, but I learned long ago not to anticipate it. I used to ask him to let me know when he got to work since his job sites can be a distance away, but the sweet gesture dwindled away. He always forgot, even when I reminded him before he left.

His father owns a pretty reputable construction company winning bids all over the United States. After John, Brian's father, saw how sedulous his work ethics were, he gave Brian a foreman position when he was twenty-one. It was a pretty big deal to us. Brian had worked his ass off for his dad for years, and he had always thought it was futile. Lo and behold, John had been watching the whole time.

Brian didn't start working for his dad until after he graduated from high school. When I met him, I was seventeen and he was only a few months older than me. It was a Friday night and I had snuck out with some friends to go to a party. I wasn't a goody-two-shoes, but I wasn't a bad kid either despite sneaking off sometimes. I was a straight A student and education meant the world to me because I knew one day I was going to go to college to have a credible job, like lawyer or something of equal importance. I hadn't figured it out yet. Although sometimes my actions were reckless, I was very responsible, which always led me to be the DD.

Brian was in the kitchen with a group of his friends, mostly from the soccer team, standing around the little liquor-filled island, laughing and cutting up. My little "clique" of friends were in the living room with a direct view of the hunky jocks in the kitchen. I hadn't paid much attention to anyone coming and going, or moving around us. I was sucked into the gossip stories being swapped between the girls. Occasionally, a loud boisterous laugh cutting through the blaring music caused us all to look up and around.

I'm not sure how we caught each other's attention, but afterward, we shared several flirty glances. A slow song over the radio finally made him advance toward me. Before he asked me to dance, he grabbed my hand like I was his to own. I wasn't about to argue with him. He was the best looking guy at the party and he was interested in me. Of course, I said yes. I'd be a dumbass not to.

I remember feeling weightless while being wrapped tightly against him as we swayed back and forth. We took turns firing off questions, interviewing each other. And even though he got way more questions in than I did, I was fine with it because he was interested in me and I was interested in him. He had the most intriguing and intense brown eyes, his black hair was trendy—cut short with bangs gelled forward—and his smile...Gah, that smile was encircled by the most enticing lips I've ever seen on a man.

After the song, we found a quiet corner and continued to get to know each other. He lived in the town butted up next to ours and was on the varsity soccer team for his high school. We exchanged numbers, told dumb jokes, laughed and smiled a lot.

Once it was time for me to leave, he wrapped his arm around my neck and kissed me very sweetly and sensually, but without tongue. I was so baffled about it. Tongue meant the guy really wanted you, like *really* wanted you. I was awfully confused and as my friends and I were walking out the front door, I glanced back thinking he had probably moved on to the next girl. Instead, he was watching me and winked. It might have caused butterflies in my stomach, but it did absolutely nothing to calm my doubtful thoughts.

Was I not a good kisser? Was I just a nightly fling of some sort? A phone number for bragging rights?

I didn't have to wait long for my insecurities to be knocked out of the park. After I had gotten home, and almost asleep, he texted me. I sprang up and smiled like a giddy little girl at the simple words: *Hey, Riley. You up?* That was the beginning of a three-hour text conversation. It was shortly after four when his replies stopped.

He apologized the next day about falling asleep and then asked me on a date. My parents were okay with me dating, but they always had to meet the guy first and I was fine with it since my dad had super powers of weeding out the jerkfaces. He could tell if they were a good catch or not by giving them a passive-aggressive third degree and only forbade me to date one guy. I was so frustrated at the time, but turns out, the guy was a weirdo and only wanted sex. How do I know? He impregnated two girls in a three-month span.

Brian was nervous to meet my dad, but not as nervous as I was. I wanted so badly for my dad to like him because this time, I was going to go against whatever he said. Brian was my one. I knew it.

And when Dad and Brian hit it off, I wanted to cry from the sheer joy I had. But I didn't. I held it together.

He took me to Olive Garden in his black Nissan Titan with tinted windows, loud stereo system, and big tires and wheels. I felt so freaking cool. No one I knew had rides like this. We all, including me, were stuck in our beat-up, hand-me-down Hondas. You were really something if you had a new car.

During our date, he made me feel special. It was all about us—school, soccer, job, parents, friends and what we dreamed our future would hold. We found out a lot about each other and one thing in particular we learned—we really freaking liked each other.

He couldn't stay out late that night because he had something to do with his dad the next morning, so after we ate, we ended up getting lost in our conversation in the parking lot for about an hour, continuing to connect. He played a gentleman the whole time until we got to the stop sign just before my house. That's when he leaned over, pulling me closer, and gave me the best kiss I have ever experienced to this day. He managed to pull exhilaration and a deep affection from every limb of my body. Hell, even days afterward, it left a lingering sensation on my lips. This was instant attraction. Instant love.

Between school, work, and him playing soccer, we weren't able to see each other again for a full week after our first date. Even though we talked every evening until the wee hours of the night, or exchanged texts any chance we got, it was torture not to see him.

But the next weekend, it was official—I was his girlfriend.

I felt like a newfangled love-drowning-puppy. I was completely in love with him.

I only worked ten to fifteen hours a week, part time as a waitress. My parents made me get a job so I could pay for my gas, but as long as my grades were good, they paid for everything else. Brian's parents were just about the same way, minus him having to work. All he had to do was keep his grades in tip top shape, not miss any soccer practices or games, and they paid for everything. He was the kid we were all envious of—didn't have to crack open a book or put in any effort to get an A.

I did manage to go to most of his practices and all his games when I wasn't working. I was head over heels for him. So much, I gave him my virginity after dating only three months. Yeah. Goodbye to the big "don't have sex until you're married" plan I had. But I was beyond ready for him. After all the making out, touching, and learning what drove us crazy, he had me throbbing between my legs daily. Hell, just thinking of him sent pulses of heat slamming into my center.

At first, he took things slow and easy, patiently allowing me to get a grip on the uncomfortable but blissful adventure. I had always heard people say how badly it hurt, so I braced for the worst. But it wasn't unbearable and I didn't experience half the shit I heard in the horror stories. He was thrilled he took my virginity and I was happy to give it to him. After we got our first time out of the way, we found a way over and over, any chance we got to have sex again—his truck, my car, quickies when our parents weren't home. We couldn't get enough of each other.

One night, his parents had a function out of town and we collaborated a plan. I told my parents I was spending the night with my friend Wendy, but I ended up at his house instead. I had dreamed of the night we could sleep in the same bed and wake up beside one another. Just like any other time, we wasted no time shredding clothes off and getting our sexual fill of each other.

This night was different, though. Normally, we did it the same ol' ways—him on top or me on top. That night, he told me he wanted to try new things with me and damn if he didn't. Doggie style started off unpleasantly and it hurt like hell, but it soon changed and I was all but

10

crawling the walls, screaming his name. Brian took matters in his own hands, flipping me around, and moving me where I needed to be—after all, he was the one with experience, not me. I tried so many new positions and did so many new things.

I don't specifically remember how many times we had sex that night, but I still very clearly remember the sheer panic on his face after he found out the condom had broken.

You sometimes hear about people getting lucky—having accidents during sex without consequence. It's like Mother Nature gifts them with a "Get Out of Jail Free" card because they endure so much fear. Typically, they learn their lessons and do everything to ensure it doesn't happen again. I'd like to tell you we were that couple, but life decided to throw us a curveball. For us, it only took one mistake and I was staring at two pink lines.

My parents lost their minds. Mom deemed me a whore and Dad saw me as the biggest disappointment he'd ever faced in his life. "We didn't raise you like this," Dad yelled at me. Mom tried talking me into an abortion or giving it up for adoption, but when I disagreed with her, Dad stepped in and tried forbidding me to see Brian again. I actually laughed. What further damage could come from seeing him? I loved Brian and no one was going to keep us apart, especially not now that I was pregnant.

I was kicked out and disowned. Shocked was an understatement. I never in my life thought my parents were capable of it. I was their daughter. I *thought* I had supportive parents. I learned they were only supportive if I abided one hundred percent to their rules. I'd held a part-time job since two months after my sixteenth birthday, worked hard for straight A's, but it wasn't enough when their daughter made a mistake. In Dad's eyes, this mistake was unforgivable.

Even though Brian's parents were highly pissed, they allowed me to stay with them until I could figure out what I was going to do. I know in the backs of their minds, my parents were going to calm down and let me come back home—no such luck.

After about two-weeks of staying with them, enduring the quick snide remarks and ugly eyes, Brian had finally had enough with all the weirdness and rented a little house just outside of town. By then, he was working full time for his dad and making really good money.

Our little house was perfect. We decorated it, fixed up the nursery, bought everything we needed, and when it was done, we sat back looking proudly at our little accomplishment. But I found out he did things much differently than I did. He used the bathroom with the door opened, had to have showers every night and every morning, tossed his clothes on the floor beside the hamper, drank out of the milk jug, and always put his dirty dishes *on* the counter. It took us a little bit to get through the bumps, but I learned to fight the right battles and not press the little ones.

One night I brought up marriage in general since we had never talked about it. And although we were young, I knew I wanted to marry him. This was when he shared that he didn't believe in marriage. My heart broke a little. He must've seen the confusion and hurt in my eyes because he wrapped his pinky around mine and stated his version of vows. There wasn't a ring. No paperwork to prove it. No excited friends or family. Nothing. But he was my husband and I was his wife.

Several months later, my water broke in the middle of the night and after ten hours of labor, they finally rested Lucas in my arms, squishy and crying. Brian was ecstatic, beaming from ear to ear and although tired, I was just as elated. I finally got to kiss the forehead of the little guy who enjoyed kicking my ribs. He was perfect and I was in love.

After Lucas was born, Brian began working more and more because he wanted me to stay at home with the baby. Brian bought us our first house—the one we still live in today—when Lucas turned one. Many glorious memories have been made here. And here is where I've watched the Brian I fell in love with change.

"Did you hear me?" Lucas says loudly.

I jerk, twisting around to him and spilling my coffee on the counter.

"You didn't hear anything I said, did you?" Lucas gives me a small smirk.

I shake my head. "I'm sorry, sweetie. I didn't."

"Where do you go when you zone out?" he asks. "I go to the soccer fields, or college or sometimes driving..." he trails off resting his head on the palm of his hand.

I smile at him. "I go everywhere."

Chapter 2

Brian strolls through the door just after I put my finishing touches on dinner. It's almost dark. So much for early...

He kisses my cheek out of the force of habit. "Give me five minutes and I'll be ready for dinner."

He doesn't wait for a response before walking off. It's not much later, I hear the water rushing through the pipes.

I grab all the plates and tell Lucas to go wash his hands while I get supper ready. Since I was young, it's been instilled in my mind that the woman always scoops up the first plates for her family, and it's a tradition I still follow to this day.

I'm setting Lucas' plate in front of him when Brian steps back into the kitchen with his black hair wet and messy. Water droplets are speckling through the gray fabric of his shirt, causing black dots to emerge randomly. He grabs a beer from the fridge and takes a seat at the end of the table.

"How was your day?" I ask, trying to kill the silence at the table.

Brian's eyes brighten and he looks to Lucas. "The biggest backhoe I've ever seen helped out today."

"No way! Did you take picture?" Lucas beams.

"I did. I'll show them to you later."

Lucas scoots his chair back and plops his foot at the edge of the table. "Check out my new shoes."

Before I can scold him for having his foot on the table, he drops it and slides back up to the table.

"They're pretty cool. I like them," Brian tells him.

"You're coming to open house with us, right?" Lucas asks with hope.

I catch the split second pause from Brian. "It's tomorrow, right?"

Lucas nods. "MmHmm."

"I'll see what I can do. I thought it was a different day."

Inside, I cringe. I hate when he lies. I've reminded him since last week and even dropped another bug in his ear last night.

Brian has never cared to be involved in Lucas' schooling. He says it's my job to keep up with it. For someone who used to thrive on perfect grades, you'd think he'd ingrain that in Lucas. But, no. It's my job and he shouldn't have to worry about it. I'm not sure what changed him—if it's the stress of bills or him being our only bread winner. Quite frankly, we're not hurting for money. He's done a damn good job building a comfortable foundation for us, but if me getting a job will relieve some of the stress and keeps him from working all the time, I'm willing to do it. Unfortunately, if I bring it up, he gets irate.

After dinner, Lucas impatiently helps me stack the dishwasher and then runs off to check out the pictures Brian took of the backhoe. Lucas is enthralled with heavy equipment, has been since he was four or five. Brian became his hero when one day he snuck Lucas onto a backhoe and let him operate it for a few minutes. You couldn't wash the smile from his face that day.

Taking advantage of the fact Brian is on the couch instead of the recliner, I send Lucas off for a shower and then settle into Brian's side.

"I missed you," I tell him softly.

"You saw me this morning."

I shake my head. "I still missed you."

He smiles and then kisses my forehead. "Missed you too." That has no emotion behind it.

I run my hand up his chest. "Is there any way you can make it to his open house. It's fifth grade. Last year of elementary."

"I can try, but don't get your hopes up."

I drop my view to my hand, frowning.

"Last year of elementary? Didn't he just start kindergarten?" He chuckles. "He's growing up too fast."

"You're missing a lot of it," I tell him honestly.

His eyes turn chilly. "Because I have obligations at work. Besides, you want things, I want things..."

"I just want you and Lucas," I say.

"It'll get better," he gruffs.

I sigh and push off him. "You've said that for years."

"And I've meant it every time." He pulls me back into him and kisses my lips softly. "One day it'll happen. Right now, I have to prove to Dad I can run the business when the time comes."

"Don't you think he already knows this? You've worked your ass off for years. Shouldn't he by now already know you can take care of things?"

Gently, he squeezes my chin. "I love how you have so much confidence in me."

"I know what you're capable of. I'm sure your dad does too. Maybe take a few days off and spend some time with us? He starts school soon."

"I can't right now. This project is important, but after it's done, we'll plan a trip. Sound good?"

Heard all this before.

I pull my lips tight and act like I've not. "Yeah. I'd like that."

Lucas comes bebopping in. "Can I stay up and play Xbox?"

Brian looks to his watch. "One hour. At nine thirty, it's bed time."

We taught Lucas at a young age if he complains or huffs, he'll lose the very thing he's asking for. Generally, he adheres to it without objections.

As Lucas heads to his bedroom, Brian leaves me on the couch and finds his way to the recliner to watch his favorite house flipping show. This is our "normal." I often joke about how we resemble a couple very late in age, but Brian is always quick to reply how good we'll look doing it after years of experience. Is this what the end of my days will look like? Distant husband ignoring me while I read on my e-reader?

It's nine thirty and Lucas returns to tell us good night. I sigh a little heartbroken. He's right on the cusp of not being affectionate with us. Most morning hugs are still okay, but not the bedtimes ones. Those have changed to unaffectionate knuckle bumps, destroying the loving mom inside of me bit by bit. And even though kisses are out of the question, I'm still able to get away with kissing him on top of the head. He doesn't seem to pay those any attention. Tucking him in isn't "cool" either, and when I try telling him no one will know, he promptly reminds me that *he knows.*

My little boy growing up breaks my heart...

Not long after he shuffles off to bed, I announce my bedtime and make my way to the bedroom, cutting off all the lights and locking the doors behind me. I change, brush my teeth, and wash my face before stepping out of the bathroom to see Brian has made himself comfortable lying on top of the covers in just his boxers and watching the television.

I bite my lip with wicked intentions. Slowly, I crawl up his body, dragging my hands over every inch of bare skin, trailing my tongue across his waist line and across his nipples up to his neck.

"You're so sexy." He grips my hips and pulls me into his erection.

Straddling him, I rock against him, splaying my hands over his chest. Quickly, he twists me to my back and presses himself between my legs. He kisses me hard, running his hands up my ribs and kneading an aching breast under his palm. I sigh quietly as he drags his lips down my jaw and nibbles on my neck while pushing his hand below my shorts. The moment his fingers make contact with my clit, I arch into his hand.

"You're always so wet for me." He nips my nipple through the fabric of my shirt.

He pulls me up and takes off my shirt and then pushes me back on the bed to do away with my shorts. His hands creep up my legs, gently massaging, and when he takes my clit into his mouth, gripping my hips, I buck and thrust into his face.

He inserts his fingers and I rock into them, moaning. Heat overcomes my body as he laps and flicks my clit, shoving deeper into me. I'm on the cusp of coming, my body about to explode when he stops with a menacing chuckle, raking his hand along my body and then shimmies out of his boxers.

Only the tip of his dick is pressed against my entrance. "You're already throbbing." He exhales and then advances the rest of the way in.

It takes my breath as he pumps into me, rocking his body against mine. Threading his fingers with mine, he places my hands beside my face and continues to drive into me. My hips push and pull with him and my orgasm centers itself to explode.

"Tell me," he says huskily. "Tell me, Riley."

His pace picks up and he begins burying himself deeper.

"Tell me," he growls, squeezing my hands harder.

His eyes are wild, dilated from arousal. He sucks in a breath with each plunge.

Tension flows down each limb, fluttering heat along with it and my orgasm springs to life. "I'm coming." I finally release the words he's been waiting for.

It floods me with scorching heat that spreads from my stomach out to my fingertips causing my eyes to roll as I shake uncontrollably from the wild waves crashing into me. Fiercely, I grip onto his hands.

"Yes, baby," he groans. "Yes. Yes, baby. Fuck, Riley." He loses his rhythm barreling into his own release.

He juts his hips, pushing himself further and groaning toward the ceiling.

It doesn't take long for him to slow, his movements becoming still when he drops to his elbow with his mouth to my ear. "I love how you look when you're unraveling."

I can't respond. I'm still clinging to the side of the cliff I just fell off from.

He slides back into his boxers and drops to his back throwing his arm over his eyes. "Such a damn perfect way to blow off steam." His tone drips with a dismissive satisfaction like I was just some random hookup he needed to get through the night.

I jerk my head toward him a little revolted at the lack of passion. "That was to just blow off steam?"

"I had a rough day," he says unconcerned with my reaction.

"And here I was thinking you wanted me," I say through the sting of his words. "Do you ever want me just to want me?" I ask as my throat tightens, fighting back the hurt.

"Of course," he sighs.

"When?"

He turns his head, removing his arm off his eyes. "All the time."

"Doesn't feel like it. I'm always initiating it or like right now, you're making it sound like I was used."

"If I didn't want you, you wouldn't get any." Attitude drips from his lips. "I could've turned you down."

I push up to my elbow. "Seriously?" I ask, surprise lacing my hurt.

A shithead grin slides across his shithead lips. "Yeah."

I gasp at the sting of his words and scramble out of the bed. "What happened to the Brian I fell in love with?"

"Oh my God. This again? I shouldn't have touched you."

I slam my legs in my shorts and rock back on my heel. "If it's a fucking struggle to be with me, why are you here?" I throw up a finger interrupting his words. "You used to love me indescribably. You used to look at me with loving eyes, spoke with loving words. I was your everything. Now, I'm only needed for sex when you've had a rough day. I don't get your loving touches and words anymore unless it benefits you. I don't know what the hell has changed, but it sucks. And more importantly, it fucking hurts."

I glare at him as I snatch my pillow off the bed and then rush out of the bedroom, quietly shutting the door behind me despite how badly I want to slam it and knock everything from the wall. I don't expect him to chase me down and apologize. He'll never do that. It's not in his blood and hasn't been for several years. Besides, I don't want him to. Lately, he lacks compassion and his words will only hurt my feelings.

I have no clue what happened four years ago, but whatever it was changed him completely. I'm convinced he cheated on me and is living with his guilt, allowing it to erode his soul. Over the years and with little results, I've tried talking to him and explaining the subtle changes, but he doesn't see just how horribly he's changed. I've been told numerous times everything is my fault. I'm the one who has changed the most, but he can't give me any good examples.

I toss my pillow on the couch and flop down, wrapping the blanket around me. Sounds of my heart thundering block out the silence and I nuzzle harder into the pillow. I ache from the pains of our ghostly love. I've learned to live in a one-sided relationship and it's sad.

Chapter 3

This morning, no words are spoken. Even after I make his coffee, I don't get a kiss, a thank you, an I love you, or a goodbye. He never looks at me to see my heart shattering as I watch him leave. I want so badly to chase after him and tell him I'm sorry, but I can't find a good reason to apologize, so my feet remain cemented to the floor beneath them.

I know he loves me, but I wish I knew what the problem was so we could fix it. If he'd only talk to me, we'd find a way. Instead, we're stuck at a painful intersection.

The school is bustling with moving bodies. Parents and children, teachers and helpers all litter the hallways. Even though the school learns from the previous years and implements new methods, this place is downright chaotic. Unsupervised children run the halls along with impatient parents who know where to go and are plowing through the new, uncertain families.

The gym has several designated areas with large signs directing our path. Lucas and I have already gotten his bus information, paid for the gym clothes, and now we're waiting, stuck in a long line to receive his class information.

"Hey, Lucas," a young girl's voice calls from behind him.

I turn and am greeted by Natalie and her mom, Patricia.

Lucas sighs under his breath. "Hey, Nat." He shakes off the annoyed tone and pulls out a fake smile.

He's been friends with her for many years, but the crush she has on him has nearly ended it. Lucas used to like her, but that was back before she started a rumor about him kissing her and being her boyfriend just to get back at another girl who also had a crush on him. He told me it was an ugly trait for Natalie. I couldn't have been more proud of him for realizing it.

I smile politely at Patricia. "You'd think after all these years they would figure out the open house woes."

Patricia laughs her "I'm too good for you" laugh and tosses her black hair off her shoulder. "You know how I feel about this school."

Mentally, I roll my eyes...or at least I hope I did. She always bitches about the school—how reckless they are, and how she despises the less than luxurious ways of doing things. She's loaded with money, thanks to her Corporate America husband, so I know she can afford putting Natalie in private school. The only thing stopping her is the thirty-minute drive there. Hire a chauffeur....

"I love this school," I say. "It's small, which allows it to give ample amounts of attention to each child. I believe it's the reason why they have such high grades. If you—"

I'm just about to give her my unrestrained thoughts when April slides beside me with her son Josh, saving me from wasting my breath. "Did you bring the wine?"

I exhale relief turning my back from the dreadful snob. "Did you bring the glasses?"

April peeks over my shoulder. "She's gone. What was the complaint today? Air too humid for her Botoxed face?"

I roll my eyes. "No one is parting the waters for her."

I'm just as thankful Natalie went with her mother. I feel bad for the girl, having her mother's snobbery ways ingrained in her brain. She's going to grow up just like her. I'm assuming she knows how Josh and Lucas are when they get together—a crow bar is needed to separate the best friends. We all became friends through soccer, meeting during practice. I immediately clicked with April due to her sense of humor and "take no shit from anyone" attitude.

She had recently divorced, but her ex-husband, Jeff, would occasionally come to practice. I'd see them sitting together, laughing and in a good mood, so you could only imagine my shock when during one of our first conversations she told me they were split. Movies make out divorcees to hate each other, but I had the opposite in my face. They didn't have hateful words spewing from their mouths. In fact, they were all good and nice things. They explained how they both knew they couldn't continue to be married or they'd end up hating each other. Their opposite personalities clashed along with their different life goals, so instead, they split and held onto the friendship.

"Oh well. I can't believe she still allows Natalie to come to this school. We're full of horrid imbeciles," she says with a twisted English accent. "Brian working?"

"Yeah. He's got a big job with an ugly deadline." It's half a lie. It *is* a big job, and they *do* have a deadline even though they're ahead of it.

Her eyes hold a deep pity for me, and she blinks it away before gently pushing Lucas on the shoulder to get his attention. "Who are you hoping for this year?"

"Anyone but Mrs. Dalton," he replies.

"Dude, me too!" Josh adds his two cents.

"I'll quit school if I get her," Lucas tells Josh.

"Remember, if you drop out of school you have to get a job and support Dad and me."

His eyes thin with indifference. "I can't do that, Mom, I'm ten." I swear a ditzy "whatever" would've amplified that better.

I smile victoriously. "Then you might want to rearrange your agenda if you do get her."

Lucas huffs, glaring at me with playful frustration, but turns his attention back to his best friend and starts whispering.

Finally at the front of the line, the older red-headed lady, who I've seen many times walking the halls, thumbs through the papers and hands us a stack with a tired smile. "Mr. Bratcher. He's on the fifth-grade hall, past the blue lockers, third door on the right." She points the direction.

Lucas impatiently waits for Josh, excited to find out if they're in the same class, and it's only confirmed when Josh jumps and rushes to Lucas, exclaiming it is.

I'm looking down at the papers when a pleased hum from April pulls me to glance up. My lungs constrict, forcing all the air from them. A sudden heat swarms my skin, and my feet anchor to the germ-infested tile floor. Tall and slender, brown hair with light streaks killing a pompadour haircut, with scruff along his jawline—he's wearing a light blue button down with sleeves rolled up and tight slacks. He's not built like a fantasy, but he's devastatingly handsome.

He looks to Lucas with a smile before his light hazel eyes, heavy with green, land on me. I have no words. My brain has tossed aside all ability to think straight.

"Hi. I'm Mr. Bratcher," he says placing his hand out for me to shake.

"I..." My mouth dries up as I struggle to remember the English language I've known my whole life and taken for granted. "Lucas' mom?" It comes out as a question and April pokes me in the back to help kick start my brain. I shake my head and take his hand. "I'm Riley," I finally get out. "You're new here."

"Yes. I just moved to town. This is my first year."

"That's good." Even though our hands have quit shaking, we remain holding hands. "You'll love the school," I tell him, quickly pulling my hand back and landing back in reality.

He licks his lips and sets his jaw into a smirky grin. "I already do."

Three words and I swear my panties just burst into flames.

He rips his gaze from me and focuses on the boys. And I swear a twinge of jealousy pangs my chest.

"What's your favorite subject?" He looks between both boys.

"Math," Lucas replies.

"Naptime," Josh jokes.

Mr. Bratcher chuckles. "Good news for you." He points to Lucas. "I have a sneaking suspicion you'll like my way of teaching math." He frowns looking to Josh. "Bad news for you. I flunked naptime. I'm no longer allowed to teach it."

Both boys laugh.

"Go in and find your desks," he says. "Fill out the paperwork with your names on it. A few pages are for parents."

The boys rush in but I'm on shaky legs staring at the floor as I pass by Mr. Bratcher. The scent of his cologne collides within the walls of my brain—fresh and spicy, smooth and powerful, radiating sexiness without an effort. I quicken my steps to put some distance between him and me.

"What was that?" April whispers.

"What was what?" I answer playing dumb without looking at her. I can't. I know heat has traveled to my cheeks, and I may or may not have drool on my lip.

Out of the corner of my eye, I watch her brown eyes home in. "Don't act like that was nothing. I saw that. Hell, everyone felt that. The Earth just shifted on its axis."

I giggle glancing to her. "Are you sure you didn't drink too much wine before coming?"

She's in the middle of saying something when apprehension weaves through every fiber of my body. "Oh no. He's in trouble."

April chuckles, shaking her head beside me, staring at the boys celebrating their desks being side by side. "Oh, he's going to learn the hard way."

This is trouble waiting to ignite as the two biggest class clowns compete in an arm's distance, the jokesters feeding off one another.

Lucas hands a few papers over his shoulder continuing to yap to Josh about how this year is going to be spectacular.

"You're going to avoid my question?" April pries again.

Determination runs in her blood. It's defines her curiosity. Even if it's just a simple reaction, if she wants to know something, she's going to get it.

I raise a brow pretending not to know what she's talking about, praying she'll drop it until we get out of here. I'll be better able to handle the questions and hopefully have a better idea of how I'm going to answer her when we get out of this classroom. She's—

"You're going to play that game?" Her tone is heavy with sassiness. She rocks back on her heels, narrows her eyes and gives me a little bitchy smirk. "Two can play that game," she says quietly before yelling out, "Mr. Bratcher? I have a question."

I want to punch her in the nose... Humiliation and shock seep onto my face.

"And that is?" he asks approaching us.

She holds up the small stack of papers. "Do these need to be filled out now?"

He points to a yellow piece of tape: Bring back first day of school.

She covers her mouth with just the tips of her fingers. "Oh! Silly me. I didn't see that."

I want to crawl under the desks.

She smacks my arm. "I can't believe we missed that."

I shake my head, rushing to my own defense. "I saw the note."

A slow smile slides across his lips, tightening the soft skin. "Busy evening. I get it." Although I know the statement is meant for April, his eyes are glued to me.

I'm overcome with an intense nervousness. "Come on, Lucas. Still gotta feed you."

I need an award for completing that sentence since wording hurts to comprise right now.

I'm desperate for air.

Just as we get to the door, Mr. Bratcher says, "It was nice to meet you, Mrs. Shepard. I look forward to seeing Lucas on Monday."

"Miss Stallings." I correct someone for the first time in ten years. "And I'm sure he feels the same way."

Something in his eyes flares and it causes jolts of butterflies to bounce off the walls of my stomach. My feet are starting to feel heavy again when thankfully, he turns his attention to April and Josh, wishing them a nice evening.

The air in the hallway is fresher than what was being stolen from me in the classroom. I take in slow and steady breaths relieved to be walking away from the small torture chamber of pleasure. I'm not even to the end of the hallway when something compels me to look behind me. I do, and my heart dips. Mr. Bratcher is watching me with curiosity, leaned against the door frame relaxed with his arms and ankles crossed.

Quickly, I jerk back around.

"Was he looking?" April asks quietly, peering at me out of the corner of her eye.

"What are you talking about?"

"Do I need to turn around?" she quips.

Ugh! "He was," I tell her.

Nothing else is said as we make our way out of the school, weaving through the crowd and into the parking lot. The boys take off running, competing to see who will make it to my car faster, when April grabs my arm and stops me.

"Are you and Brian okay?"

"Of course," I tell a white lie through my teeth and she knows it. "Why?"

She glances to the school and then back to me allowing a knowing smile to dominate her features. "Whatever *that* was in there—"

"*That* was nothing," I interrupt.

She studies me with a stern look, like I'm a child being busted for lying. "You can pretend as hard as you want that fireworks just didn't explode between you two. I know what I saw."

"You're seeing things because there weren't any fireworks," I say and then stride off. The last thing I want to do is admit and explore what *that* truly was.

Irritation launches when we pull into the driveway to see Brian is already home. Lucas and I both enter the house at the same time, and he darts off to his dad in the recliner with several papers scattered across his lap.

"Why didn't you come to open house with me?" Lucas bites.

Nonchalantly, Brian points to his lap. "Had a few things to finish up. How was it?"

"If you had come, you would know," Lucas bites again, but this time with repercussion. Brian hardens his stare, silently warning Lucas to drop the attitude without words. You can clearly see that Lucas wants to obliterate Brian for being at home and not coming. He stands there mentally debating it until he finally comes to his senses and stands down. "I have a new teacher. He's cool."

I set my purse on the counter and begin making dinner as Lucas tells Brian about the afternoon. Since I'm making spaghetti— simple, easy, and quick—it's not long after starting it before I'm scooping up everyone's plate and calling them to the table.

Brian twists his noodles and looks up to me. "Seem like a good teacher?"

It's the first time he's acknowledged my existence since we've been home.

"If you had come..." I shake my head, deserting the argument that's sure to follow the sentence. "Yes. He seems like he'll do well, except he's going to learn the hard way about sticking Lucas next to Josh."

"You left that part out. He put you beside Josh? Is he crazy?" Brian teases Lucas.

"We won't get in trouble," Lucas beams wolfishly.

"You best hope not," Brian warns. "You don't want to mess up at school and let it trickle home and into soccer."

Lucas doesn't respond, scooping food onto his fork and taking a bite.

Right after supper, Brian makes his way back to his self-made desk. Since there isn't much conversation, Lucas takes a shower, plays a little bit of video games, and then goes to bed. With no reason to stay at the end of the couch as an invisible object, I decide to take my e-reader to the bed with me.

I'm comfortable—changed, pillows propped up, covers tucked around me—but my mind is everywhere except in this book. Every sweet or sexy thing the male character does causes images of Mr. Bratcher to flash behind my eyes. Every edge and curve of his face, every wrinkle and line of his clothes against his skin, his deeply saturated green hazel eyes...I hadn't realized I carved his image into my memory.

"What are you thinking about?" Brian's voice screeches my thoughts to a halt.

I jump, startled. I didn't hear him come in. "What? Nothing. This book is interesting," I blabber.

He narrows his eyes. "Uh, huh."

I hold up my e-reader. "Romance. It's sweet."

He slides into the bed, turning off his bedside light and lies with his back turned toward me.

This is the aftermath of a pissy Brian, one I learned about many years ago. Pissy Brian holds onto his frustration and feelings much longer than he should. I used to do whatever I could to help him snap out of it—sexual favors, favorite meals, sweet little presents—but it didn't take me long to realize I was always the one giving in and I got tired of it. If I do any of those now, I have to be in a really special mood. Tonight isn't one of them.

I reach over and shut off my light, place my e-reader on the nightstand, and curl up onto my side.

I wonder if Mr. Bratcher holds grudges for long.

Mentally, I shake my head at where my thoughts are continuing to go. Today was a page torn from the spine of a romance book and I was the main character. Who knew stumbling for words or falling short of reality actually happened in real life? I've never experienced anything like it—only read about it.

"You have to look at the book to read it," Brian says into the darkness.

I hold my breath as my heart slams into my chest and a bubble of laughter tries making an escape. I got busted daydreaming.

Chapter 4

Lucas started school a few weeks ago and ever since, I spend my days cleaning the house, keeping laundry tamed, reading, and crafting. I enjoy making little things. It helps me keep my sanity. Just recently, I tried something new and now I'm completely addicted to paper quilling. Who knew rolling up narrow strips of paper would be so fun and relaxing? The other day, I found a heart on the internet and thought how fabulous it would look on the wall separating the kitchen and living room. I couldn't wait to get started on it and now, I'm almost finished with it.

Lucas will be home shortly, and as I slide all my paper strips into a little shoebox I've decorated for my crafts, my phone alerts me to an email from Mr. Bratcher requesting a parent teacher conference tomorrow evening. School's only been in for a few weeks, so this can only mean one thing—Lucas has gotten into trouble. I sigh and respond just as the brakes from the bus squeal, announcing Lucas' arrival.

He springs through the door with aggravation written on his furrowed brows. "When you went to school, did they have homework?"

I laugh. "Hello to you too."

He throws his book bag on the table and it lands with a hard thump. "Mr. Bratcher gave us vocabulary words. Hard ones. Big ones." He drops into his chair, rips open the zipper, and yanks out his binder. "I mean really hard ones."

"You want to get smarter, don't you?"

"I'm ten. How smart do I need to be?"

"Some ten-year-olds have already advanced to college."

He rolls his eyes. "With all this I'll never keep up with soccer."

"You said the same thing last year. Remember how you never thought you'd make it through fourth grade? You haven't even been in school for a month yet. You'll figure it out and fall into a good routine. I'll help as much as I can."

"That was a breeze. But this..." he chucks his paper down in front of him and it slides hitting his book bag, "is much different. Times have changed since you've been in school."

"I wasn't born in the nineteen hundreds, son. It hasn't changed that much," I tell him with a laugh.

"Did they have desks when you went?" His disposition finally changes and he lightens up with his joke.

"We sat in something that looked like church pews as little Johnny slid on the floor beneath us to pass notes," I jest.

He laughs, reaching for his paper, but his adorable little smile melts away as he tries pronouncing the first word. "Gig...an...tic."

I peek over his shoulder and put my fingers over part of the word to help him break it down.

"Gi...gan...tic. Gigantic!" He looks to me surprised.

"Ah. Not as hard as you thought, huh? You know all these words, kiddo. Just break them down and sound them out. Do all the ones you can and I'll help you with the rest."

I gave him the confidence boost he needed because he finishes all the words quickly and without my help. But one thing is for sure, Mr. Bratcher is going to get a kick out of the sentences Lucas put together. *I'm going to make a strategy to end all homework.*

I head outside with Lucas and watch him kick the ball around. Soccer practice will start soon and, of course, he's excited about it.

When Lucas was born, Brian no longer played but still had the love for it. Once Lucas started walking, Brian taught him how to kick the ball, even though it was more Lucas' foot running into the ball as he clumsily tried taking steps. But once Lucas got just a little bit older, Brian had him in the backyard teaching him the basics. They would stay out there for hours and before I knew it, Brian had instilled the same love he had for soccer into our son. Unfortunately, it wasn't long after, work consumed Brian and he doesn't come out here often anymore.

Lucas kicks the ball straight to me and instinctively, I stop it. "Come on, Mom, show me what you got."

I purse my lips. "Nothing. Absolutely nothing and you know I don't."

He talks me into it anyway even though I'm horrible at it. My kicks have no direction and I send Lucas chasing the ball every time. Don't worry, he purposely returns the favor. Needless to say, I'm about to die from all the running.

You'd think with all the soccer love in this house, I'd know how to play. You'd think wrong...

Chapter 5

The school is quieter than during the day as I pass under the humming lights toward Lucas' classroom. Only a few teachers remain with different groups of children participating in their afterschool activities. Soon, Lucas will be one of those kids, staying after twice a week for practices.

I swallow hard when I pass by the blue lockers and enter the classroom. Mr. Bratcher is at his desk clicking away at his computer when he notices me and grins.

He stands, pushing out his chair with his legs. "Miss Stallings."

Navy blue doesn't do his eyes any justice.

"I've got us set up over here." He strides to the tan half-moon table by the back of the room. "Where's Lucas?"

"I didn't know if I needed to bring him or not. Sort of figured he was in trouble." I sit and place my purse on my lap.

He sits across from me with several papers in his hands and shakes his head. "He isn't in trouble. A lot of parents worry whether their child is adjusting well and I like to relieve them of that concern with an early sit down. After this, I'll only do conferences when requested and with every report card. If you're ever unable to make it to one, I can do it over the phone as well."

As he's been talking, I've taken in every swooping strand of his hair, every moving muscle in his forearms, and the way his lips shape around each word.

"Okay," I say.

His eyes hold a curiosity lit by attraction as the left side of his lips pull up, assaulting me with the sexiest smirk I've ever seen in my life. "Where would you like me to start?"

Oh, the dirty thoughts...I clear my throat, trying to rid myself of them. "Wherever you prefer."

He delves into all the things every proud parent wants to hear. Lucas listens well, participates often, and turns in his assignments completed and on time. He's adjusting well and excelling. He extinguishes any concerns I have about the two boys sitting beside each other, explaining how they actually add to many of the discussions and how they unbelievably are not causing any disruptions. Which is surprising since last year they spent more time in the principal's office than class and they weren't even sitting close.

"He's really a great kid," he concludes folding his hands on the table. "I think I went over everything. Do you have any questions?"

I don't know if he went into perfect detail or if I'm still stuck in a stupor, but sadly I'm at a loss for words. I shake my head. "I think you've covered it all."

He raises his left eyebrow, dropping the right one so strongly it shades his eye.

But just then, a question finally wiggles out from the depths. "Lucas will be starting soccer soon and it will dredge into his homework time during the week. Last year the teacher gave homework on Monday and expected it back on Friday. Lucas hasn't said what your schedule is."

A small flicker flashes in his eyes for a brief second. So minute that if I had blinked, I would've missed it. "Normally, anything he doesn't complete in class should be finished as homework and turned in the following morning. I won't accept anything after class starts. Vocabulary words are given on Monday and expected to be turned in Thursday. I don't assign many, ten to fifteen at the max with definitions and a sentence using the word. Shouldn't take too long."

Lucas knows soccer will put a strain on school work and if his grades start to slide out of control, we'll rip him from the sport. Thankfully, so far, he's done great at balancing everything.

"I don't know what superpowers you hold or if you're just an extremely patient man, but I'm warning you, keeping him and Josh so close could turn into your kryptonite," I state with a small laugh.

He grins. "The boys actually work really well together. And the times when they're clowning around, they're only adding flavor to my lessons instead of hindering them."

"You're a brave man, Mr. Bratcher."

"Call me Trenton." His tone drops to a sexy low.

Suddenly, there isn't enough air and I scramble to my feet. "Thank you, Mr. Bra-Trenton." I correct myself. "I'm glad Lucas is doing well for you. He has nothing but nice things to say about you."

He pushes to his feet, flaunting a victorious expression like he just received an answer to an unasked question. He sticks his hand out for me to shake. His hand is warm and a little sweaty as he gently squeezes. A pulse jolts me, this time in my chest and my breath snags, getting caught somewhere in my throat. I jerk my hand back and stumble backward.

"It's, um, thank you," I jabber nervously adjusting my purse strap on my shoulder.

"Thank you for coming, Riley."

The way my name falls from his lips like he licked every damn letter that exited his mouth causes a shiver and my mouth falls open. I turn, praying my feet will quickly get me the hell out of this classroom when he calls out behind me.

"These are yours." He launches an alluring smile, one that's gorgeous, sexy, flirty, and downright kissable.

What the hell has come over me?

I take the papers without looking at him and rush out.

I wish I knew why he had this effect on me. Every time I get around him, I tumble over my bottom lip, my thoughts get jumbled, and I don't hear a damn thing. I'm completely unable to concentrate while watching every movement his body makes like it's the last time I'll ever see them.

Lucas knocks on the car window and I screech, grasping my chest.

He's doubled over in laughter when I push open the door.

"How long were you going to sit in the driveway?" he asks through his cackle.

It's contagious and I begin giggling. "You scared the hell out of me."

"That was epic!" He snorts.

I wave at Clarissa, a sweet older lady who watches Lucas from time to time, and head toward the house.

"What'd Mr. B. say? I'm not in trouble, am I?

I narrow my eyes. "Well," I start, sounding as if something did go down. "He did tell me that you..." I stop. Curiosity always gives me the power I need.

"What? He said what? What! I've been good," he frantically scrambles out.

I chuckle, placing my hands on his shoulders. "He said you were an excellent student and a joy to have."

Under my palms, his body relaxes and he starts in the house.

Earlier today, I threw the ingredients to chicken fajita soup, one of our favorite meals, into the crockpot and when we push open the front door, the delicious aroma bombards us. The whole house smells amazing.

I kick off my flip-flops and fish my phone from my purse to give Brian a call and find out when he'll be home.

"Yeah?" He started this crude, unaffectionate greeting years ago and I've hated it since the first time I heard it.

"Hey, baby. Just wondering what time you'll be home and if I need to wait on you for supper or not."

"I'll, uh..." he pauses saying something muffled by his hand to someone else. "About two hours. Start without me."

Inwardly, I sigh. "Okay. I love you," I say.

"Yeah. Love you too." And he hangs up.

They're apathetic words I wholeheartedly despise worse than the unsentimental "yeah." When these emotionless words started making a presence into our everyday conversations, I blamed it on "a guy thing," but truth be told, he used to say them with such a deep affection regardless of who was around. I feel like I'm owed a loving mannerism instead of dull obligation.

It's after nine thirty and I'm in the bed watching a show on tiny houses when Brian finally comes home and heads straight for the shower. Since things haven't been good between us lately, I can't help but have untrusting, doubtful thoughts and I loathe that I do.

I pop my head into the bathroom. "Would you like for me to warm you up a bowl of dinner?"

He finishes washing his face and then wipes the water from his eyes. "No. I grabbed something on the way home."

"Oh. Okay."

He opens the shower door wide enough to shoot me a warning glance. "If you're going to start bitching—"

A hurtful anger settles between my shoulder blades, but I bite my tongue. Quickly I shake my head. "I'm not. It was a long day. I figured you'd be hungry." Why I sit here and try to be nice is beyond me.

He shuts the door and I slide out of the bathroom back into the warmth of my covers and continue to watch the show about tiny houses. These things fascinate me. I'd love to live in one, or at least give it a shot, but I'd have to wait until Lucas moves out.

Brian comes out in his boxers and crawls into the bed, leaning over to give me a weak kiss on the cheek.

"Will you kill the TV? I'm beat and I wanna go to sleep."

"Did you have a bad day?" I'm grasping for straws to spend some time with him.

"No. Just long." He rolls over with his back toward me.

"Do you think you could ever live in one of these tiny houses?"

He chuckles. "The walls would close in on me. It would be like living in a shed."

"Some of them are really nice."

"Doesn't mean I'd want to move into one."

"I think it would be neat after Lucas moves out," I tell him.

"Don't expect me to join you in your midlife crisis journey," he states unmoved by my opinion.

I turn off the TV and roll over. "What if I got a burgundy Harley Davidson? Would you join me then?"

"If I got my own, sure."

"You won't ride on the back of mine?" I try asking straight-faced and without a giggle, but I'm unsuccessful.

"I'm more likely to get a motorcycle or a Lamborghini than to move into a fancy jail cell. Don't spend your time dreaming of these tiny houses. I'm not moving into one."

Of course it's all about you, I want to say, but I don't. I leave it alone knowing I have at least ten more years to change his mind.

Chapter 6

Yellow and blue uniforms scatter across the field. Kids holler encouraging words to their team mates while they practice their drills, and others cut up waiting for their turn at running the ball. The coach is shouting directions and blowing his whistle. It's hot, sweaty, and humid. Yep. It's officially the start of soccer season.

I've parked my butt in my hot pink chair to the side of the bleachers where I can still see the kids. Lucas' soccer playing is much different than Brian's was. He's more laid back and less intense. Brian, on the other hand, was extremely intense and wildly competitive. But I believe in the next few years, he'll start to resemble more what Brain was—manically enthralled.

The new coach orders the kids to begin running passing drills. He's watching them intently so he can get a feel for their skill levels. At the beginning of practice, he got all the kids to introduce themselves and say why they're playing. When it came to his introduction, he was very straightforward. He's here to coach and better them in soccer. If you're not here to practice, learn, and play the sport, don't waste his and everyone else's time. If you don't listen, you'll be on the bench. If you talk back, you'll be on the bench. If you disregard the safety rules, have unsportsmanlike behavior, or deliberately try to injure another player, you may not make it off the bench and back onto the field. And his frank warnings weren't just for the children. He also gave us parents a warning. If we get out of hand during practices or games, our child will suffer the consequences.

He's an older man with age shimmering in every line of his face. His chin juts out and his nose is crooked like it's been broken before, but he's clean cut. Coach Porter—I already like him better than the flimsy coaches from the past few years.

The whistle blows and he pulls a few of the kids out of the passing drills and starts them on dribbling. I used to think this was easy. I used to think it was something natural. That's until Brian had me try it in his backyard once. I ate the ground big time. I lost my footing, tripped over the ball, and landed flat on my face. Easy? Looks can be deceiving...

"Why are you hiding over here?" April asks, dropping her chair beside mine.

"It's hot in the sun. I have shade here."

"You could've told me. You left me out there for the mom wolves," she deadpans.

"How many years have we sat in this very spot? Don't blame me because you wanted to chit chat with all of them." I point toward the other parents.

"You're right. I was looking for someone to replace you." She snorts.

I toss my head back in laughter. "You could never replace me."

"Doesn't stop me from trying." She smiles.

Being best friends, we thoroughly enjoy a good banter and giving each other a hard time.

"I like the new coach," she says. "He's pretty candid."

"It's just what the boys need. He sounds like he wants them to go to the Olympics."

"At least he'll weed out the kids who don't really care and focus on the ones who do. I think it's going to be an interesting season."

Thirty minutes of practice remaining is all that separates me from the cold AC of my car. I'm wiping the sweat from my brow when something catches my eye from across the field and causes a funky racket in my chest. He's striding up the bleachers taking two steps at a time and sits in one of the empty rows across the top, directly in the blasting path of the afternoon sun.

"Ooh..." April sings, nudging my elbow. "Hottie at twelve. Wait? Is that Mr. B?" She pulls her sunglasses down her nose.

I pretend I haven't seen him and scan the bleachers. "Where?"

"Top middle," she says.

"It is him," I say like I've just spotted him.

She glances at me over her sunglasses and then shoves them back up her nose. "I didn't feel the ground shake. Wonder how long he's been sitting there."

"I'm sure he just got there."

"You've been watching him," she says knowingly. "I bet he is sitting there to watch you."

"Why would he watch me?"

"Why wouldn't he?" she replies.

"Why do you always answer my questions with the same questions?" I chuckle.

"So he hasn't spotted you?" she giggles mischievously. "Should I grab his attention?"

"No!" I quickly scold, grabbing her arm and preventing her from doing anything humiliating. "Don't. He might get the wrong idea."

"Now we wouldn't want that, would we?" Facetiousness laces her tone as she playfully cuts a shit eating grin and shoves her tongue into her cheek. She settles back into her chair. "You have to admit, he's pretty hot."

"He is very handsome," I answer honestly.

My view shifts from Lucas to Trenton and then back to Lucas many times. I've lost my focus. I pull my sunglasses off and squeeze the bridge of my nose, trying to relieve the pressure the sunlight has given me. Too much of it has always been the quickest route to headache-ville. You'd think by now I'd be used to it...

I open my eyes to Trenton staring directly back at me. This isn't one of those instances when you wonder if someone is just looking in your general direction. This is very clear. He smiles and throws his hand up in a smooth wave. Dummy me, waves back. Guess whose attention I just got?

April clears her throat compelling me to quickly shift my view to Lucas. "He's very friendly," she says.

"I agree. He spoke very highly of Lucas and Josh at the parent teacher conference this week."

"He's already having those?" She sounds surprised. "I didn't get anything about it. Did he send a note home? Dammit, Josh. I bet it's at the bottom of his book bag."

"No. He sent out an email."

"I didn't get one." She pauses. "I bet you're the only one who did."

"What? That's ridiculous."

She scoots to the edge of her seat. "You know how I hound teachers for Josh's information and updates. If he was setting up PTCs, I'd be the first to know."

It's my turn to pause because she's one hundred percent right. She always knows about these things before I do...always.

"I think he has a crush on one Miss Stallings," she practically sings while she slides back into her chair. "Something as fine as him. You're one lucky bitch."

"What if it's you he's crushing on? What if it's you he just waved at and I looked like a dumbass waving back because it wasn't my wave to wave at?"

She laughs loudly. "What the hell did you just say?"

This makes me giggle too. "He could've been waving at you."

"You're flustered and it's making you grab at straws. Own that shit, Riley. He's hot as hell and checking you out. Pull your shoulders back and own it. You may be married." She air quotes the word. "But you're not dead."

I glance back to Trenton and catch him staring at me, but he quickly pretends to be following the ball...on the other end of the field.

I settle back into my chair and rest my arms on the flimsy arm rests. "So it's okay to think he's gorgeous?" I ask without looking April's way.

"Mmm hmmm."

"Is it bad I sometimes think of him randomly throughout the day?"

"Not a bit."

"Does this mean there's trouble in paradise?" I ask, but I know the answer.

"There's been trouble in paradise for a long time. *This* has nothing to do with it."

I sigh and she pats my leg. "The man in the bleachers has nothing to do with the problems Brian brings home. He just gives you something pretty to look at. It's natural to fantasize, Riley."

Embarrassment floods my face. "I don't think of him like that!"

The whistle blows and I jump clean out of my chair to my feet.

April is in stitches, gasping for air through her cackle.

I fold my chair while the coach has his last words and then watch Lucas grab his bag and jog toward us.

"I like him," my little boy squeaks out of breath. "'Bout time we got a good coach. I wish Dad was here to meet him."

"He'll meet him soon."

He pays the comment no attention and we start walking to the car with April and Josh.

"Dude. He's gonna kick our butts," Josh says to Lucas.

Lucas turns around and walks backward. "Maybe we'll have a good team this time."

"I hope. We can't keep on keeping the team up," Josh replies and April laughs.

"What's with all the bizarre sentences today? First Riley, now you. Is it in the air? Is it contagious?"

I elbow her arm. "For the record, Josh and I make perfect sense."

"To who?" April snorts.

Josh chuckles and opens his mouth to reply when Trenton calls out from our left. "Good practice, boys!"

Both boys yell out a "thanks" in an excited unison as he approaches us.

His lips quirk up and it instantly swarms my body with a bubbly heat. "Hey, Riley."

"Hey, Trenton." I act like he doesn't give me butterflies and continue walking to my car, desperate to put distance between us.

"First name basis..." April leaves the statement dangling out in the open. It's a trick and I'm not falling for it.

It's killing her that I'm not taking the bait and as we say our goodbyes, she murders me with her wry stare.

We're both surprised to see Brian's SUV sitting in the driveway when we pull in. Lucas barely waits for me to put the car in park before he springs out of the car with his bag and runs into the house.

"At first, I thought he was gonna be a total jerk, but he means some serious business." I hear Lucas telling his dad when I enter the house. "I really like him. I think he's gonna be good for us."

"I always enjoyed getting a good coach. When I was a sophomore, we got a new one. Coach Clark. He was incredible and I looked up to him. He busted our butts in practice, but winning the championship made all the hard work worth it."

"Did you get a scholarship?" Lucas asks innocently.

Brian cuts his eyes to me. "I could have, but I quit playing after I graduated."

"Why?"

Brian leaps to his feet and puts Lucas in a headlock, giving him a noogie. "Because of you, you little turd," he teases. "I'd rather have been a dad than a soccer player."

Lucas wraps his body around Brian's leg and fights to take his dad down, but Brian doesn't budge. Realizing there isn't anything else he can do, he let's go and slides down to the ground and looks up. "Can you become a coach? You could coach our team. I can be your assistant!" He scrambles to his feet.

"Fat chance, kiddo. Go take a shower. You smell like eight-day-old socks."

They both laugh as Lucas lifts his arm and waves air from his arm pit before rushing off.

"You used to smell just as bad," I tease.

"I disagree. I smelled much worse. I don't know how you put up with it," he says.

"Vicks VapoRub," I state. "Slabbed it in my nose."

Playfully, he frowns. "You used to tell me I smelled sexy."

"Oh, you did. Just like menthol," I snort. I pull out the hamburger patties and hand them to him. "Care to cook the burgers?"

He glances back to his makeshift office and then back to me, but before I allow another work excuse to spill from his mouth, I cut in. "You can do that after supper. Fix the burgers." It wasn't a request but a polite demand.

His lips pull tight. "I hate I'm missing his practices." He takes the patties.

"You'll make it to the games, right?"

"I hope." He strides out the door.

I've heard that before, too. He won't. He hasn't in two years. I swear he says these things just to calm his guilty conscience, but he doesn't realize he's becoming a broken record with empty and hopeless promises. His words fall unreliable. He never sees just how much he's actually absent from our lives.

Chapter 7

Today is a scorcher. I've tucked my chair as far into the shade as I can get it while still leaving room for April. She texted me earlier and said she was running late, but I just saw her pull into the parking lot.

She hurries across the grass, her brown hair flowing in the wind she's creating from the speed of her steps. When she reaches me, she opens her chair and drops in it out of breath.

"Did I miss anything?"

"No. They've just been running different drills."

"Good," she sighs. "Work ran so far over today. I absolutely loathe firing someone. I displace them and throw their world upside down, and then there's the pile of paperwork I have to fill out afterward. I know that sounds bad." She rolls her eyes. "I'll never get used to releasing someone."

She works in the HR department for a big-time clothing retail store, which is why she's always dressed to impress and wearing the hottest and latest trends. I have rarely ever seen her dressed down. She's always in pretty blouses, nice pants or shorts, and the best-looking shoes. Occasionally, at home, she rocks out in yoga pants, but you'd have to sneak in on her to see it.

"Was it deserved?"

"We don't have a huge turnover rate and we don't enjoy firing for the fun of it. So, I'm sure."

My brows pinch together. "You don't know the reasoning?"

"I do, but what I'm told versus the exact truth may not line up."
She takes a deep breath, rolling her shoulders backward. "What are you
doing tomorrow evening?"

I shrug. "Not sure. Why? What's up?"

"Duck's is having a wine tasting and I want to go. Come with
me."

"Duck's? Isn't that the bar downtown?" I ask.

She nods. "That would be it."

"Isn't it weird for a bar to have wine tastings?"

"They have them all the time. It would be a different story if it
was a bar-bar. But this is a classy, elegant bar. They serve wine and
calamari. Coming or not?"

"I'll have to check Brian's schedule," I tell her.

She shakes her head. "Have Clarissa watch Lucas until Brian
gets home. No excuses. You need a night out."

God, she's so right. "Yeah, I'll ask her and run it by him
tonight."

I can tell she has a lot on her mind. She's not her normal lively
self, and when I try picking at her, she doesn't arm herself with ammo
and come back with anything. I allow the silence to take over, and even
though words aren't shared, her company keeps me content.

I'm livid. I've made dinner, called Brian twice without an
answer, and now I'm cleaning in anger. My thoughts are everywhere—
he's in a ditch, flipped over, knocked unconscious, off the side of a cliff
with no one able to see him. Anxious thoughts are a bitch...

Lucas has already taken a shower and done the little bit of homework he had. Now he's playing a soccer game on his Xbox. Even in the gaming world he's addicted to the sport.

I'm scrubbing the same invisible spot with all the elbow grease I have when Brian comes in from the back porch. I snap around, aiming my cleaner, ready to shoot my intruder.

He throws his hands up with a smirk. "Easy, Miss. I'm just passing through," he states in a cowboy southern drawl.

"Where the hell have you been?" I snap.

His eyes snarl. "Nice to see you too."

"It's late and I've called you twice."

He pulls his phone from the clip and swipes the screen a couple of times. "Shit. Fuck! I forgot to turn the sound back on after our meeting at noon. Fuck. I've missed a shit ton of important calls."

My emotions are on high alert. Hurt, fear, anger...they all intertwine, braiding into an irate woman. "Do I not ever cross your mind?"

"You do." He walks past me and pulls open the fridge.

"Why wouldn't you call me when you know it's getting late? A courtesy call to ease my worried thoughts."

"You know my hours are all over the place right now." His tone holds no emotions.

"Which is a better reason for you to pick up the damn phone and let me know what's going on. A text. A call. Something, Brian!"

"Sorry." That was the hollowest apology I've ever heard.

"Yeah. That you are," I sneer, tossing my rag on the counter.

"This is exactly what I enjoy coming home to after a long day. A bitch."

Murder chokes his neck when I home in on him. "Don't you dare point blame to anyone else but yourself. *Our* lives revolve around *you*. We don't know when you're coming home, what days you have to work, or shit about your schedule. I think asking for you to consider *me* for a moment isn't too much to ask."

"You can do whatever it is you wanna do without worrying so much about me."

Hot tears threaten my eyes but I blink them back. "I'm sorry I give a damn about you and want to include you in the plans of *your* family. I'm also so fucking sorry that I worry because I love you."

I storm off and up the stairs. On my way to the bedroom, I poke my head into Lucas' room and tell him to hit the sack. And then I draw a long hot bath, lock the bathroom door and sink into paradise. Although, I'm pissed off at him, I'm trying my best to keep Brian out of my thoughts. I focus on my breathing, the water around my skin, and the smell of the vanilla candles beside the tub.

I've stayed in the bath long after my fingers have pruned and the water has lost its sting. I dry off and change into my pajamas before opening the bathroom door into a pitch-black bedroom. The light behind me illuminates, channeling into the darkness and showcasing Brian in the bed with his back turned to the spot where I would lie.

I grit my teeth and make my way to the bed, sliding under the covers and turning with my back toward him. It's a position we promised years ago we'd never lie in on purpose. Funny how loving words can be so easily broken.

"You over your shitty attitude?" he asks with more anger than he should carry.

I let out a breathy, frustrated laugh but don't say anything. I don't want to argue anymore. I want sleep to lull me away from reality.

"I didn't know you tried calling," he says, again with way too much anger.

"You didn't think to call me," I state.

"You're right. I didn't."

Tears swell and pour from my eyes. "Thanks for showing me how much you love me."

"I'm still here, aren't I?" he asks, his tone infused with disdain.

That stings. "Wow, Brian. Just fucking wow. Please don't stay if you feel forced. I'd much rather have someone who wants me instead of obligated to me."

"I'm both." And for the first time tonight, I hear the honesty in his voice.

"You're more balanced on one side," I say angrily and then bite my lip knowing my words are starting to take stabs. I sigh. "Good night."

Chapter 8

I didn't speak to Brian this morning. We shared no words. He didn't apologize. I didn't apologize. And when he left, we didn't say we loved each other or share a goodbye kiss. The air between us was concentrated with animosity.

Last night, through the blurry blackness of my tears, I deemed tonight to be an eye-opener. I'm going with April without telling Brian. If he doesn't want to make an effort to call me, then not knowing what I'm doing is his fault. And when I don't answer his calls, he'll understand my daily worries.

I still haven't heard from him when I drop Lucas off with Clarissa and head over to April's house a few roads away. I knock on the door and almost immediately she pulls it open, strutting a shimmering silver tank top with a beautiful design and matching earrings topping black skinny jeans and a gorgeous pair of black heels. Suddenly, I feel way underdressed.

Her brown eyes slide down my body and she smiles widely. "Look at you! I haven't seen you this hot in...damn! I'm impressed."

I'm nothing as spectacular as she. I've got a tan half-sleeved shirt covering a white, loose flowing tank top, a pair of jeans with rips and tears, and nude heels. My hair is half pulled up and my makeup...well, it's the same. I'm not as classy as her.

"I didn't know what to wear." My grand entrance of word choice.

She grabs her clutch and keys from the table beside her door. "Take a breath. I know it's been a while since you've been out. Just breathe."

I do—in through my nose, out through my mouth. "I'm fine. Trying something different tonight."

We slide into her fancy little black Mercedes. "Different like how? New panties? Sexy new bra?"

"Brian and I got into an argument last night and he said some pretty hurtful words."

"What happened?" she asks keeping her eyes on the road.

"He came in late *again*. I was already mad, so I snapped at him for not calling me and that's where it started. His reply was for me not to worry so much about him, and as petty as it sounds when I say it out loud, that shit still stung. He even had the audacity to call me a bitch."

"A pissed off Riley. Haven't ever seen her. Maybe being alone made you grow some balls."

"I think the better term would be depleted, or maybe deflated. I don't know." I shake my head. "I just wish I knew what the hell was going on."

"Is he cheating on you?" she asks.

"What? No!" I answer hastily. "Why would you think that?"

"He's been closed off for a while, coming home at all different times, and he's never around."

I fall quiet allowing her words to settle into my brain. Would he cheat on me? Could he? I've had my doubts before, but I figured they were purely insecurities from the circumstances.

She reaches over and pats my leg. "I'm not trying to put thoughts in your head. He's a good guy. Just like you said, he's just working really hard. I'm sure having a boss who's also your dad breathing down your neck is straining. He's got big shoes to fill."

"I know he's stressed out, but I should be his solace, not someone he comes home to and bullies to make him feel better." I sigh, resting my head on the back of my seat.

"Let's loosen up," she says and then punches the button to her radio. Music fills the car, along with our laughter and our poor attempt to sound incredible.

She's perfect at lightening up the mood.

The pub is slammed. She failed to mention they were still operating a Friday night schedule during the wine tasting. And by wine tasting, I mean you can order a glass of wine and taste it as you drink it.

"I knew if I told you I just wanted to get you out of the house, you wouldn't have come," she says with bright doe-like eyes. "You needed this. Sue me for loving you." She holds her hands up in an exaggerated surrender, giving me the best "you can't argue with me" grin.

I purse my lips displaying the weakest scowl. "I hate when you're right."

She winks. "You'll thank me later."

From the large front window, night has fallen onto the streets. This isn't a huge dance club with a DJ, strobe lights and loud music. Instead, the bar is separated, split into two main sections. On one side is for dancing, with a wooden floor where several people have already made their way out. And on the other side, the side I'm on, is the bar, which is much quieter. I'm perfectly fine, swaying from foot to foot talking to April as she man hunts.

Brian and I didn't have time to hit up the clubs with our friends when we were younger. Normally, once every two or three months, when we found a baby sitter, we would grab dinner and either end up at the movies or at a friend's party. The bar scene was never our thing.

I've been slowly nursing my beer, when suddenly, someone hands me one from behind. It takes me a moment to register what's going on as I stare at the levitating beer, being held only by the palm of a large hand.

I take a step away before I turn around. "Trenton?" My breath escapes me.

"Need a beer?" he asks with the most beautiful smile.

I take it. "Thank you." I furrow my brows. "Are teachers allowed to go out and drink?" I quip.

"Are moms?" he shoots back playfully. His eyes scan me, from my wavy chestnut brown hair all the way to my nude pumps. "You look good."

Heat spreads over my cheeks. "Thanks."

"Hey!" April says stepping up beside us and eyeing me suspiciously. "Mr. B, I didn't know teachers got out to drink."

I raise my brows and smile victoriously. "See. I'm not the only one who thought that."

He chuckles. "Yes, ma'am. We're allowed to have lives, just quieter ones."

She steps between us and slams her finger into his chest. "You call me ma'am one more time and I'll cut off your nipples with a spork."

I burst out laughing, pulling her hand away.

Trenton clears his throat. "What would you prefer me to call you?"

She sticks her hand out. "I'm April."

He shakes it.

She flicks her eyes between him and me. "I'm going to purr my way over here. I'll be back in a few."

Before I can protest, before I belt out to not leave me alone, she's gone, sucked into the crowd without a trace of her existence.

Nervously, I glance back to Trenton. "She refuses to believe that ma'am is a term of endearment, not disrespect." My voice quivers a bit and I try hiding it with an awkward breathy laugh.

"I was raised to call everyone ma'am and sir. I have a strong suspicion my nipples may be cut off more than once. And why a spork? That's kind of sadistic."

"She doesn't get out much," I jest.

"Now I see where Josh gets his sense of humor."

"I'm sure you haven't seen the best of it yet. Wait until he gets really comfortable around you."

"Lucas is quite the jokester. I can't wait to see what he brings to the table in the middle of the year."

"If he gets out of hand, you let me know," I reply more seriously.

He shakes his head following a pull from his beer. "Nothing I can't handle. I was the class clown when I has his age. I haven't met my match yet."

"Don't wish for it too hard," I say.

"Care to dance?" he asks with a gleam of hope in his eyes.

I shake my head and scrunch my nose. "No, thank you. I'm not very good at it."

He tips his head to the dance floor. "It's a slower song. I'll keep my distance like a middle school boy." He exhibits by holding his arms stick-straight out in front of him.

This makes me laugh.

He scans the room. "April is out there. We'll slide in right beside her." He places his beer on the low table beside us. Again, I shake my head. "Come on," he says with a sweet grin.

I give in.

He tucks his hand under my elbow and leads us to the dance floor. Just as promised, he stops beside April, who has taken up with a man in his early forties with black hair, a plaid shirt and jeans. He's got a hell of a grip on her waist as they dance, but she seems to be comfortable as she laughs and smiles up to him. When April finally notices us, her face lights up and if possible, her smile grows wider.

I laugh when Trenton does exactly as promised and keeps me at arm's length with his arms straight and his hands on my waist. I slap him in the arm, dropping my head back as I laugh. He wraps an arm around my waist and pulls me closer, leaving enough room where our bodies aren't touching.

I haven't danced with another man in years. For that matter, I haven't danced since prom. Brian doesn't do much dancing. He isn't the romantic type even though he used to be. Everything used to be.

"This okay?" Trenton's eyes question me.

I bite my lip, suddenly feeling more shy, and nod. I feel like I'm doing something wrong even though I know I'm not. But I'm in the arms of another man, and I know if the tables were turned I'd be irate. But for some reason, in this very moment, I don't care.

We dance at a distance, to a song that isn't too slow but not fast enough to twerk around the dance floor. It feels awkward because we're not doing much talking as we sway from side to side, and once the song begins to end, relief cascades around me.

April's man pulls her tighter and whispers something in her ear that causes her to giggle that flirty, breathy laugh she's practiced for many years. The next song is slower than this one.

"You realize you're stuck with me until this song ends?" Trenton says blithely.

I offer a polite and nervous smile. "Okay."

I feel so out of my element. I don't know what to say or what do to. I'm stuck, moving side to side with his hands resting just above my ass. I feel brittle, like one step, one slight rush of breeze and I'm going to shatter with pieces of me getting lost under everyone's feet.

"Why do I get the feeling you're uncomfortable?" he asks.

"I'm nervous," I admit truthfully.

"Your nervousness is killing my confidence. I'm at a loss for words."

"I'm really sorry. It's just been a long time since I've danced."

"You couldn't tell it. You're doing well." He grins. "What do you do for a living, Riley?"

"I'm a stay-at-home mom," I tell him.

His shoulders tighten below my hands. "I...I didn't know you were married."

I roll my eyes. "I'm not. He doesn't believe in marriage."

His hazel eyes swirl with questions. "How long have you been together?"

"Eleven years."

His eyes widen. "That's a long time to commit to someone and not marry them."

Hello, embarrassment...

"I think he's crazy not to," he murmurs.

"Can we get off this sour subject?" I ask.

He looks me dead in the eyes with an alarming shimmer of hopefulness. "Not really. This subject decides my next subject."

I open my mouth to say something, but I have nothing. I blush maddeningly. I drop my view to the black fabric of his shirt...speechless and unsure what to say.

"That was pretty direct. I'm sorry." He leans closer to my ear when I don't look up. "I'm sorry."

"It's fine," I tell the shirt, melting at his breath on my ear.

"Can I be honest with you?"

I nod.

"I'm a little heartbroken now."

I flick my eyes to his.

"Someone who looks as exceptionally great as you within my arms reach and I find out you're taken," he answers my unasked question. "I never see you with him."

I want to groan. "Yeah, well, me neither." My tone is way more hateful than I mean for it to be.

"Why's that?"

I stop dancing, removing my hands from him. "Thanks for the dance. But I need a drink."

His demeanor changes. His eyes are frantic. "I didn't mean to upset you."

"You didn't," I tell him and then turn walking away.

He strides in step beside me. "At least let me buy you another beer for ruining your night."

He motions for the bartender and orders us two beers. I grab mine and immediately take a long swallow from it. I'm humiliated by Brian and he isn't here. "Thanks," I say. I'm hollow.

"I'm not really good at this," he says leaning his elbow against the side of the bar.

"Now you understand why I'm not either," I say with a dry attitude. He physically flinches and I feel badly. "I'm sorry. It's just..." I shrug. "I'm disappointed I've been with the same man for eleven years and no one knows it. I have nothing to show for it except an exceptional child. He doesn't care to spend time with Lucas or me." I shake my head. "It's frustrating I'm always alone."

"How long has it been this way?" He looks genuinely concerned.

"Years," I answer flatly. "I'm sorry. I'll quit." I just unloaded a ton of unhappy troubles into Trenton's lap, and this pity party has shown me just how dispirited I truly am.

He tightens his lips. "Apparently, you needed it."

"Yeah," I sigh into the open. "I need to get April. I'm ready to leave. Thank you for the dance and the beer."

I stride away as he sits back and watches me. I'm ready to end the awkwardness and brace for the inevitable I'll see when I get home.

"Where the fuck have you been?" Brian springs out of the recliner toward me.

Inside, I smile. "Out with April."

"You didn't let me know."

I set my clutch beside my purse on the island. "Was I supposed to?"

"I tried calling you," he grits.

"Yeah?" I open my clutch and pull out my phone. "I didn't know. I wasn't paying attention."

His expression darkens, creating angry creases across his forehead. "So what the fuck were you doing that you couldn't answer my calls?"

I smirk, devilishly. "Last I was told, I could do whatever I wanted without worrying so much about you. I don't see what the problem is."

He zeros in on me with an evil hostile glare. "What a childish act. How fucking old are you?"

I don't answer, reaching into the fridge for a bottle of water.

"You went out of your way to make me eat my words. Are we back in high school, Riley?"

"I didn't go out of my way. April asked if I could go to a wine tasting with her. So, I did." Technically, that wasn't a lie. "I don't see what the problem is," I repeat.

He slams his hand down on the counter causing me to jump. "My working is much different than partying," he growls.

"I didn't party. Why are you so mad?"

He narrows his glare without blinking.

That's when I feel the immaturity seep into my bones—the realness of his words and the truth behind them. I feel like sinking into the floor, disappearing beneath the slatted hardwoods. The whole plan sounded perfect when I devised it, even sounded great as I told myself in the mirror what I was going to do. One thing's for sure—it's lit a fire under his ass.

"I'm sorry," I say quietly. "I didn't think you'd mind."

"You didn't fucking think."

"That's enough," I say flatly. "I get it. I messed up. Bad choices and all that stuff." I wave my hand dismissively.

His chest is heaving with wild eyes gripping me.

My imperfection shamefully turns into anger. "It doesn't feel good, does it? Sitting there wondering and worrying. Unsure what you should do or not. I might have gone about it wrong, but hopefully you'll understand where I come from now."

"You know where I'm at. Work. It's where I stay. It's where I sweat and bleed. I'm surrounded by employees, contractors, sweaty, pissy men. When I said you shouldn't worry about me it's because I'm at fucking work," he spits out.

"I try hard to include you in the family every night. I try holding off dinners, making sure your breakfast is made, texting you game times or anything that deals with Lucas. You come home after having a bad day and I *always* try making you happy, but instead you'd rather berate me to lift yourself out of your miserable hole by burying me in it. Day in and day out, I make sure you're respected as the man of the house whether we see you or not."

I hadn't noticed the tears until they run down my cheek.

"Have you forgotten it's me who keeps you up? I pay your bills and everything else around you that keeps you home even though our son has been in school for years. I'm the one working my ass off. Not you."

"I beg to fucking differ," I snap. "I may not work as hard as you physically, but I have a pretty hard job."

He throws his head back and sneers a laugh. "Sitting on your ass in the air conditioning can be pretty damn draining, I'm sure."

I wipe the tears off my cheek. "No. Having a busy child can be pretty draining, but you wouldn't know anything about it."

He glowers at me, but my words are stabbing him right where I knew it would hurt.

"I offered to get a job. You won't let me," I cry out. "Do you think I enjoy never seeing you? We never get to spend time with you. Do you think I like that? I fucking miss you more than I see you."

"Stop it!" Lucas screams, shifting his eyes from Brian to me. "Stop. All you ever do is fight. Why can't you get along?" He squeaks, fighting off the emotions.

"Lucas?" I take a step toward him, but he steps backward, madder than hell.

"Don't walk away from your mother," Brian growls.

"Why? You do!" Lucas retorts.

It leaves us speechless, burning sorrow into our skin like a lit cigarette. I glance to Brian whose eyes are narrowed and glued on Lucas.

"It's bedtime," Brian states trying to sound levelheaded.

"How can I sleep with you two arguing?" Lucas snaps back.

"We'll stop," I tell him. "I promise. I'm sorry."

Lucas leaves the kitchen, stomping all the way up the stairs and into his bedroom. He slams the door behind him, causing me to jump.

"He's got your attitude," Brian says smartassed and still pissed off.

I huff a mad laugh and pull my heels off. "I'm going to bed," I say over my shoulder, leaving him in the kitchen.

"This conversation isn't over," Brian's quietly calls out.

It stops me and I turn on the ball of my right foot. "Yeah, Brian, it is."

We share a vicious stare before I turn back and make my way to the bedroom. I wash my face, change my clothes and crawl into the bed. I don't care to read, honestly. I'm mentally exhausted. I nuzzle into my pillow feeling a mixture of proud to have proven a point and foolish to have done so in such an immature way. I never thought of it from the angle Brian slapped me with. I was so enthralled with the idea, I forgot the consequences. Although, at the time, I couldn't have cared less.

I'm asleep holding on to my pillow tightly when Brian finally comes to bed. And even though he's woken me up, I pretend not to be. He clambers under the covers and lies there for several long minutes before exhaling and turning over. I shut my eyes, screwing them tightly to keep my tears at bay.

I hate this...

Chapter 9

I didn't sleep well at all last night. I woke up every time I moved in fear I was touching Brian. Yeah. That's how disgusted and mad I was at him. I didn't even want to touch the skin on his body in my sleep.

I woke up before him, came downstairs and started coffee. Thankfully, I don't have to watch the dark liquid gold fill the pot for too long before pouring myself a cup.

I'm at the table when Brian strolls into the kitchen fully dressed and pours himself coffee in his travel mug.

"I'll be back later," he announces as he strides back out.

"What?" I jerk to my feet.

But he never responds, only quietly shutting the front door. Confusion rattles my soul. He didn't grab his hard hat or any of his normal items he takes to work. I call him but am quickly shoved to his voicemail. I try again with the same result.

I drop back into my chair.

Emptiness sinks into my soul as I feel alone in the home we've created. My soul is an endless pit and my heart aches. It's pretty bad when it aches for itself. I've always heard there's a difference between being alone and being lonely, but I never truly understood it until recently. I'm lonely. Miserably lonely. Even with Brian in the same room, there isn't a connection. There isn't a spark. Our friendship is lost at sea—our intimacy somewhere in a blurred line.

It was all subtle in the beginning. I could feel everything slipping away—the "us" I knew—but I held on tight, hoping and praying it would pass. It didn't. Slowly, the little sweet things we would do for each other slithered away and instead of the loving talks, our words became sharp and bitter. It seemed like we both were out to draw blood from our words, to see who could hurt worse. It was a blood bath of words but I ended up stopping. Hurting him always destroyed me more. I gripped tighter to our long-lost dream—us together, forever, happy and a family. He let loose of his grip, settling comfortably into a heartless soul I didn't recognize.

Everything came unglued and somewhere we lost our happiness. It never mattered what I did—cooked his favorite meal, pleased him in the bedroom, kept my feelings to myself and smiled as if there were nothing wrong—he turned cold, using me for his own greedy needs. I became an object. He became a ghost.

I take the last sip of my coffee and rinse the cup out in the sink before heading up to wake Lucas. He's going to be heartbroken when he finds out Brian is going to miss yet another first game.

I tap on his door before opening it. "Rise and shine. Game day. Need to get you up and fed so you can show your superpowers out in the field."

"I'm up," he grumbles, pulling the covers over his head.

"Looks like you're lying in a horizontal direction," I tease knowing I'm riling him up.

"Ugh!" he groans.

I laugh. "What would you like for breakfast?"

"Cereal."

"Better get up soon or it'll be soggy when you get to it."

"Mean trap, Mom. Unfair."

I can't help but laugh. I'm overdramatic with it as I head down the stairs, allowing it to echo off the walls. When I enter the kitchen and grab the cereal box, I'm still laughing as loudly as I can.

He comes sliding into the kitchen. "Why do you laugh? Your evil laugh is horrible."

I feign hurt. "What are you saying?"

"You can't be the villain in a movie. Don't try out for one," he says stoic as hell.

"So, can I be the princess?"

He shakes his head. "Superheroes don't have princesses." He huffs like it was important and I shouldn't be joking about it.

"Then what can I be?"

"Mom. Just be mom," he states dryly and then shoves a bite of cereal into his mouth.

I smile. "That I can do. I'll be superhero mom."

He rolls his eyes and deserts the conversation.

Lucas' first game isn't a home game and what's worse, April isn't able to make it. You know that woman is sick if she's not sitting in the bleachers of a game. Josh came with Jeff, April's ex-husband who very rarely misses games anyway.

It's hot. So freaking hot! I'm at the top of the bleachers in the only spot where I won't be smushed between other parents, but I'm closer to the searing devastation of the sun slamming against my back. I feel like I'm on fire.

I'm watching closely, focused on the game and leaning into my elbows when I'm startled by a vanilla ice cream cone.

Trenton smiles. "Figured you needed something for the heat."

My surprised eyes falter into furrowed brows. "I'm beginning to think you're following me."

He takes a seat beside me. "When I was Lucas' age, I played. I loved the sport. When I taught at my prior school, I never missed a game. I won't change that for this school. School pride."

"People are going to start getting the wrong idea of us."

He pans the crowd. "Let them. I have nothing to prove to anyone. Besides, where in the handbook does it forbid me to befriend a pupil's parent?"

"You have the most carefree attitude," I say.

He wipes his palms against his black plaid shorts. "Best attitude to have. When you start caring what others think of you, it starts making life pretty shitty."

"The teacher cusses?" I quip abrasively.

"Why are you in a bad mood?"

I cut my eyes to him, silently warning I'm definitely not in the mood.

"He's pretty good." He nods toward the field and I'm assuming he's speaking of Lucas.

"It's been instilled in his brain. His dad used to play," I tell him.

"Play by his own choice?"

This warrants a confused expression. "That's an odd question. But yes. He used to love it."

"Strange he is never here to support his son since he used to love it and is the one who taught Lucas to love the sport."

I wrench my head in his direction. "That stung."

He spreads his hands. "I didn't direct that toward you, Riley."

I stare at him in disbelief before exhaling. "I'm not in a good mood."

"I can tell. You should smile more," he states allusively.

"Do you always flirt with your students' parents?"

"No. Just you. Most men don't like it when I tell them they're pretty."

I laugh.

He grins wolfishly. "That's what I was hoping for."

I purse my lips at him, scrunching my nose.

The rest of the game we share many what this player should have done, what the coach should do, and how the practice drills need to be focusing on each child's needs. We laugh at some of the overly exerted outbursts from other parents. But mostly, we sit quietly, in each other's company, watching the game. And when I ask why he isn't a soccer coach, he shrugs the question off with an excuse of other subjects to focus on.

He no longer flirts with me, which both relieves and disturbs me. I appreciate the respect, but after a few emotional touches, I sort of miss it.

The time ends. The whistle blows. And our team runs out, jumping up and high fiving one another. I grasp Trenton's arm and squeal, jumping up and down out of excitement. He chuckles and I grab my bag, tracking down the bleachers as fast as my legs will take me. I stop by the opening in the fence waiting for the teams to finish their game handshake. Then I wait even longer for the coach to discuss different things with the players.

"I always hated this part. When we won, I was ready to get out of there and celebrate, not get lectured," Trenton whispers beside me.

"This drives me nuts!" I whisper-yell to him.

I tap the top of the metal pole, impatiently waiting for Lucas, until the coach finally ends his damn speech. Lucas strolls up with his black bag over his shoulder, his dirty blond hair slicked back from sweat, face red from the heat, but beaming from ear to ear.

"We kicked their butts!" he exclaims.

I snicker, bumping my hip into him. "It's nice being the winner, but not so much on the losing end. Be nice."

"But we won," he groans.

"And I'm so happy and proud of you. No need to rub salt into their wounds."

"She's right," Trenton says. "Win with pride and dignity. Feel bad for the losing team."

Lucas' little face lights up.

"Good win," Trenton adds and then shifts to me. "Good sitting with you. I hope you have a good week." His gaze lingers, holding something fierce inside of it. A tingle wraps around my spine and I shudder. His left brow raises and then he looks back to Lucas. "I'll see you Monday."

As he walks away, I frown. Part of me wilts. His company has quickly become wanted. He's fun, light-hearted and he makes me forget about the desolate situation at home.

Since he won, I allow Lucas to choose dinner. Pizza it is! We're enjoying a supreme, extra cheesy pizza when Brian shows back up. I haven't heard from him since he left this morning and I haven't tried getting in touch with him.

"We won!" Lucas hollers as Brian pulls a beer from the fridge.

"That's great!" Brian sits.

No eye contact. No acknowledging my existence. Nothing.

Even after his first slice of pizza and halfway through the second, still nothing.

Frustration braids together with hurt and it bubbles deeply inside of me. As hard as I'm trying to stay composed, I can feel that I'm slowly losing the battle. I excuse myself and disappear into my bathroom for a long hot bath. It's my escape. The one place I lose myself into an oblivion. I'm there to relax and forget about all my problems.

I run the water, adding a few drops of Lavender to further my relaxation, slide out of my clothes and dip into the steaming hot water. My muscles release their tension and I rest my head on the back of the tub, closing my eyes.

Normally, I think of a tropical paradise—beach, palm trees, the sound of the waves breaking, rising and falling against the wet sand. Usually, I can see a hammock swaying in the wind, and off in the distance, I can hear the squawk of a seagull. I imagine it so perfectly; I swear I can feel the soft breeze on my face.

Not today.

Not this time.

Today, I see Trenton and all his glorious good looks. He's leaned against a wall, his taut muscled arms crossed over his buff chest. His face is relaxed, his smile pulling his sexy lips tightly as he's excited to see me. His hazel eyes shimmer with happiness. And his hair allows the wind to ruffle it.

My eyes bolt open and I'm back in the bathroom. I giggle at myself as I trail my fingers through the water and watch as the wakes ripple out toward the sides of the tub. I close my eyes once more. Again I'm greeted by Trenton, but this time he's in my hammock wearing bright orange board shorts. I rip open my eyes again and splash some water over my face.

I am not supposed to be thinking of him. He shouldn't be in my relaxing fantasy.

There's a click as Brian pushes open the door and sits on the edge of the tub.

"I'm sick of arguing with you," he says. "Something has to give."

"I agree."

"As fucked up as this sounds, work will be coming first before you both for several more years. It will get easier when this job is over."

"You say that every job," I remind him.

"I wish for it every job," he replies. "You're going to have to figure out a way to deal with me being gone, Riley."

"I wouldn't mind it so much if you could be with us every once in a while. And I mean be with us. Not sitting in your recliner, flipping through files, ignoring us and calling that family time. When's the last time you went to one of Lucas' games? Or a practice? The very sport you used to love so much that you shoved it in the veins of your son, you show no support for."

"I never have time."

"Make time."

"I wish I could," he says.

"Have you ever heard someone wish they worked more on their death bed?"

He shakes his head. "No. But right now, me spending more time with you both won't happen. I can't find the time."

"Then make the time you're home special," I say. "Where'd you go today?"

"It's not important," he tells me sternly and pushes to his feet, leaving the room.

He's ruined my mood. I get out, dry off and slide into a pair of comfy pants and a loose shirt. Brian's sitting on the side of the bed looking out the window when I exit the bathroom.

"Are you cheating on me?" It's a fair question.

He puffs. "You think I am?"

"All I know is the Brian I love with all my heart is lost somewhere in the shell of his old body. He's not there anymore. If you were, it would explain a lot."

"I can barely handle you, let alone another woman."

"Not if she's the *work* you're always at."

Time stands still for a moment and then he blinks up to me. "No, Riley. I'm not seeing anyone else." He runs his hand through his hair. "I hate you think that."

"I hate you give me a reason to think it," I admit, coldly.

"You've always had a wild imagination."

I shake my head. "This isn't creativity at its best. This is how you make me feel."

"You think things up so definitively you begin to feel them too. All this," he twirls his hand. "It isn't as bad as you're making it out to be."

"Coming from the very man who interrupted my bath to tell me he's tired of arguing. Yeah. I'm sure it's all my imagination. I'll work on that."

He sighs and then exits the room. I watch as the door shuts behind him, confused about where he meant for the conversation to go. For the past few months, this is how we talk. Quick sentences here and there, but never a resolution. Never a compromise.

I'm always left with an open wound, hurt, broken, and uncertain where we stand. I meant my words when I said he was just a shell. He's empty. I'm empty. We don't laugh. We barely talk. And there's not much contact of any sorts without anger. Even under the same roof, we can be standing in the same room and not exchange a look.

Once he used to eye me from across any room. In those very glances, I could feel the depth of his love for me. His stares would pierce my soul and I could feel his want, his need for me. But those very looks dissipated over the years.

I know he's not the only one who's changed. I have too. I've grown. I've become a mom. I've molded around his world. What crushes me the most is I feel I've become a roommate who occasionally shares an intimate moment with the man she lives with.

I tell Lucas goodnight and grab a bottle of water before heading to bed. I challenge Brian with a broken-hearted stare until he let loose of it first to go back to working. Now, I've laid here for what feels like an eternity, begging my mind to settle down and let me sleep. Finally, it agrees and pulls me into emptiness.

Arms wrap around me in the dark, lugging me out of my sleep. Brain scoots my back closer to his chest and rests his head behind mine. I clench his hands and squeeze. Unfortunately, my tears make their presence known.

"I'm sorry," he whispers. "I do love you, Ri. I don't ever want you to think differently."

"I miss you," I cry. "I miss us."

He sighs. "We'll get through it. We always do."

I swallow but it does nothing to relieve the tightness in my throat. "Please. I'm begging you. I love you. Please help us. I can't be the only one trying. I need you."

"You've always been the glue that holds us together," he says with a shaky voice.

"It's easy when you have two things that can be glued together," I gasp between tears. "Please..." I plea in my saddened cry.

His breath shakes again, but he doesn't respond.

"I love you." My whisper shakes. My body trembles from the sobs and he tightens his grip around me. "If you don't want to be with me..." I trail off, trying to catch my breath from my sobs. "This is torture," I squeak.

He kisses the back of my head and holds me tightly while I cry. And when I begin to calm down, he strokes my hair, helping me to relax in his arms and allowing me to fall back to sleep.

Chapter 10

Surprisingly, after my meltdown, Brian took off yesterday and spent the day with us. We talked during breakfast, picked and played with each other, and when he took Lucas outside to kick the soccer ball, I swallowed the lump in my throat. I hadn't seen that in a long while and I couldn't tell you how long I watched them, but I enjoyed every second of it.

During dinner, Brian didn't sit in his normal head of the table seat. Instead, he sat beside me and across from Lucas. He squeezed my leg under the table and smiled every chance he got. He even helped clean up the kitchen, and that came with flirty fun and loving kisses.

Once Lucas went to bed, we retreated to the bedroom, where for the first time in a very long time, Brian made love to me. It wasn't just sex. It was intimate love. Soft and sensual movements. Every thrust offered loving affection. Every touch offered a sense of importance. He growled how much he loved me all the way to the end, and as we lay tangled up together, he was still pouring out his feelings.

My Brian...he's back.

I'm cleaning the living room, dancing and bouncing my duster to the music when my cell phone rings.

"Hey," I answer with a goofy grin.

"Hey," Brian says. "Figured I'd call you and tell you that you're on my mind."

My chest swells.

"Also, I'm going to be late," he adds.

My inflated, filled with giddiness chest loses its swell. "Oh," I say trying not to sound so devastated. After all, this is his norm. I shouldn't expect anything different. "Everything okay?"

"Yeah. Just work," he replies monotone.

"I'll make you a plate and leave it in the microwave for you," I say.

"Thanks. Listen, I have to go. Love you," he says rushing off the phone.

"I love you too."

He hangs up.

I sigh. Even under a new leaf, there's still a sting to his words. Regardless of how much we're working together to make things better and to change our ways, the typical pattern has an ugly jab. I should be used to it, but I'll never become complacent with being unable to see the man I love.

The coach informed the kids that today will be warm ups, drills, and a short scrimmage. Everyone's faces light up, eager to get to play the short game. He places several kids in different groups and, from what I can gather, he teams up the timid players with the braver kids to help them overcome their fears.

"How are things at the homebound?" April ask adjusting in her seat.

"Better," I tell her. "Friday blew up like a grenade in my hand, but Sunday turned out to be marvelous. He actually spent time with us."

Her lips stretch widely. "Maybe a dose of his own medicine is what he needed?"

I shrug. "He was highly pissed Friday and made me realize how dumb of an act I played, but I'd do it again if these are the results."

"I hope it works. You two used to be—"

"What the hell is he doing here?" I exclaim, leaping to my feet.

I can't contain the grin ripping across my lips. My heart drums in my chest. Striding across the grass with his shoulders back and black hair bouncing with his steps, Brian locks eyes with me and smirks. I leap, wrapping my arms around his neck as he approaches us.

"What are you doing here?" I can't hide the elation in my voice.

He squeezes me. "Came to watch Lucas practice."

I find my footing. "I thought you had to work late."

He shrugs one shoulder with a cheeky smile. "I got off early."

I'm beside myself and cling to his arm as we take a seat in the bleachers beside my chair.

"Hello, stranger," Aprils says.

He tips his head. "April." His tone is neutral.

"It's good to see you here," she says trying to ignore the weirdness between them.

Brian knows I tell her things. She's my best friend. She's going to know all the good and the bad. April is a little reserved around him because she knows what I go through. Regardless of how many times she offers a fake smile and tells me she's happy we're getting along, I know she can't stand him.

"Me too." His response is clipped as he glances back to the field. "How does Lucas do with these relay races?"

"Very well."

Brian leans his elbows on his knees and rests his chin on his fists, watching...intently. "He needs to get better with turning. There's a pause."

"I know someone who used to be the next David Beckham who could teach him," I thrum.

The corner of his lips quirk, but he doesn't look over to me. "I'll give him a few tips."

He remains focused, scooted to the edge of the metal seat the rest of the time, and I think he might lose himself while the boys scrimmage for the last twenty minutes of practice. He spots all the timid players, all the mistakes the coach doesn't call, and quietly cusses the coach under his breath. I know the deep adoration he has for the sport, so I'm not about to tell him this is the best coach this team has had in a long time.

Lucas comes bounding toward us, gleaming. "Dad! You came."

Brian tucks Lucas' head into a headlock and chuckles. "You looked good out there. I hear the pros calling you now."

Lucas gawks when Brian lets loose. "That would be super cool."

"It'll happen. Especially if you keep this up." He slaps Lucas on the shoulder.

Trenton pops out from behind the second set of bleachers and calls out to Lucas. My insides flutter and immediately I'm overwhelmed by an odd sense of guilt. I've never told Brian about Trenton and Lucas' friendship, or ours for that matter.

Trenton ignores Brian and keeps focused on Lucas. "Good practice," he says. "But I saw one issue. You're heavy on your feet at times. Lighten up."

"I got tired, Mr. B.," Lucas confesses.

"Champions don't get tired. You need to do more conditioning. Try alternating between short and long sprints."

"I'm sorry. Who are you?" Brian interrupts with a condescending tone.

Trenton smiles devilishly. "Mr. Bratcher. Lucas' teacher and number one fan." He slides his hazel eyes to me. "Next to Riley of course," he states with a deep admiration.

He's being a smartass.

"I'm Brian, Lucas' dad." He puffs his chest out. "There isn't a bigger fan than me."

"Hmm," Trenton grunts, cocking a brow, faking perplexity. "Strange. I've never seen you at a practice or a game."

My eyes bulge and I grimace.

"Don't forget we have a math test tomorrow," Trenton tells Lucas and then his eyes, braided with a protectiveness and care, shifts to me and he displays a sweet smile. "I'll see you next practice."

Brian clears his throat compelling me to rip my eyes off the back of Trenton. His eyebrows are drawn in closely, his nostrils slightly flaring. "A friend of yours?" That wasn't just a caustic question. It was laced with an accusing imploration.

"Lucas' teacher. He's come to all the practices and the game." I don't lie.

He narrows his eyes and tilts his side. "Really?"

"He says he loves the sport," I shrug nonchalantly. "Let's get home so I can make dinner."

I'm dying to get out of this conversation.

"Can I ride with you, Dad?" Lucas interrupts Brian's sharp glare.

"Yeah," he says. "Go ahead and get in the truck."

Lucas has gained distance from us when Brian grasps my arm, stopping me. "What the fuck was that?" he gruffs.

His fingers dig into my skin. "What are you talking about?"

"Did I interrupt something between you two?"

I yank my arm out of his hand. "You've lost your mind," I grit. "Apparently, I'm not the only one with a wild imagination." I spew his own words at him and storm off toward my car.

I toss my chair in the trunk and drop into my car. I haven't even cranked it up when my phone rings.

"The more I'm around him, the more I don't like him. And if I ever see him put his hands on you again, I promise I won't bite my tongue," April seethes through the phone. "He was so busy demanding your attention... What the fuck just happened?"

"I'm assuming his insecurities just flared."

"Did Mr. B. say something to light the fuse?"

"Yeah," I say sharply. "He didn't act himself. He was a smartass."

"We are talking about Mr. B., right?" she snorts. "Maybe he did it to light a fire under Brian's ass?" she questions.

"For what gain? What would he possible get out of it?"

"Maybe he thinks having another man interacting in your life will benefit you? Or he was marking his territory?"

My face pinches out of confusion. "Do what? That's ludicrous. He knows where I stand."

"The other night you stood before him."

"Don't. Don't make me feel guilty for having a friendly encounter. I did nothing wrong. I laid stake where my heart is."

"Doesn't mean he's not interested in you," she says.

"I think he truly likes Lucas and Brian's absence upsets him."

"Does playing dumb help your conscience and put blinders on you?"

"Yes," I exhale the truth. "If I pretend I don't see it then it's not there."

"That only works when you're little hiding from ghosts under the sheets."

"It's working for me now. Okay? Just let me handle this how I want," I snap.

"So you do see it then?"

"It's an illusion, April. I'm starving for attention."

"So close to the edge of the truth and she jumps the hell off the cliff," she laughs.

Anger draws me in as I pull into the driveway behind Brian's Denali. "None of that was anything. Quit trying to make it out to be something. You're overreacting to a morsel of attention and looking into things that aren't there."

"Whatever you tell yourself, honey." She sounds restrained forcing a calm tone. "Call me if you need me."

Once in the house, I make a beeline to the kitchen, avoiding everyone, and start dinner. I'm vexed replaying the whole afternoon from Trenton's smart-aleck interactions to Brian's jealous responses as I cook. I'm using more force than I should as I stir the hamburger meat, and the sound of the knife slamming against the cutting board echoes as I cut up the lettuce.

I call the guys to wash up and am scooping the taco meat into their shells when I feel his eyes on me. His presence is always intense and it crawls across my skin. I turn to see Brian leaning his shoulder against the door frame with his arms crossed, watching me thoughtfully. I smile tenderly, still frustrated, and turn back around to finish making the plates.

He presses his body against my back and lays a kiss on my cheek. "I'm sorry."

I close my eyes and lean back into him.

"I hated how he looked at you," he says.

"No one can ever look at me the way you do," I tell him.

He huffs a short breath and places his lips to the shell of my ear. "I recall looking at you just like that before we started dating. I wanted you. Lusted for you. And fantasized about you."

As sweet as that sounded, the hidden insinuation makes me uncomfortable and I swallow it, twisting into his arms. "I think you were drunk that night," I tease folding my arms around his neck. "In fact, you were so drunk, you could've humped a stop sign and known no difference."

His brown eyes smile. "I wasn't drunk. And there was something about you. I didn't want to hump you that night. I wanted to get to know you. You deserved better than a heartless fuck, but if I had known you were going to make me wait three long torturous months to have sex with you, I probably would've fucked you in the bathroom."

I giggle. "It was worth the wait," I whisper kissing his bottom lip.

"Well worth the wait," he agrees with a low tone.

"I've missed this," I say.

"Show me how much when we go to bed," he whispers.

I'm in the shower when I feel his presence again. I wipe the water from my eyes and even though I know he's there, I still jump a bit.

"Lucas is in bed. He says goodnight," he states.

"Care to join me?" I ask from under my wet, matted lashes.

His eyes travel down my naked body, pausing briefly on the areas that arouse him the most. He shakes his head with a wolfish smile. "Are you finished?"

"Yeah," I answer.

He reaches in, turns off the water, and grabs my hand leading me to the bed. Cold air blasts against my warm skin and goosebumps spread. Drops of water stream down my body, creating puddles underneath my bare feet. He pushes my wet body onto the bed and gets out of his shorts, springing his arousal from the confines of the fabric.

He starts at my feet, lapping the water and gliding along my calves and up my thighs. I sigh, sinking into the wet, sticky covers. His brown eyes are fixed on mine, ignited by seduction. I writhe when he makes his way over my hip bone, crossing my stomach and traveling up to my breasts. He clasps my nipple between his teeth and gently bites down. My body reacts, my back bowing off the bed. A chuckle vibrates my skin as he trails his tongue to my neck, taking a brief pause at my jawline before making his way down the left side of my body.

Once to my left ankle, he heavily drags his hands up the inside of my legs crawling between them. He dips a finger into me, and immediately heat courses across my skin. He watches as my body takes his fingers, before leaning and tracing my clit with his tongue.

I melt against his hand, moaning softly and rocking my hips into him. Lightning bolts shoot into each limb as my orgasm begins to peak. My legs begin to quake.

"Tell me," he sighs against my apex.

"I want you," I whine, giving him the wrong answer.

He flicks his tongue hastily, sucking harder, and pressing deeper into me. It sends me over the edge. My hips thrust forward against his face, my grip on the sheets tighten, and I begin my ride off the cliff. I rock against his mouth, panting.

He clambers on top of me and shoves his dick into me, filling me as he leans and catches my moan in his mouth. I drag my hands up his cheeks and scrape my fingers along the sides of his head through his hair. Wrapping my legs around his hips, he brings his body to mine creating a marvelous friction.

"You're fucking perfect, Riley. I love you so much," he grits out between thrusts. "So fucking perfect."

He repeats over and over how much he loves me before his plunges become fierce and he shudders, losing himself into me. His hips lose control and he lets out a long groan, apologizing and begging me to forgive him.

He falls to his back, pulling me against his chest. Our breaths are wild, out of control as he drags his fingertips along my shoulder. But before I know it, we level out and his heartbeat is steady under my ear.

I play with a small patch of hair right below his belly button. "What do I need to forgive you for? Why are you so sorry?"

His heartbeat picks up in tempo again. I feel his muscles tense under me. He reaches and stops my hand, pulling it up and around his neck, adjusting our bodies where he's on his side and his forehead is against mine.

"For not being here as much as I should be," he finally answers.

"I love you regardless." I smile but something doesn't feel right. The air between us is heavy. My gut instincts are worrisome. "Are you sure that's all?"

He blinks slowly before returning this gaze to mine. "I hate how much we miss each other."

I dance my fingertips along his cheek. "You need a vacation."

He laughs softly. "That's a word in my vocabulary I miss using. It will be a long while before I'm able to."

"Maybe you're feeling sick?" I tease.

He laughs again. "Sick or not, I still have to go in."

"Not if you have a man-cold. I've heard those are pretty deadly," I jest.

He kisses my forehead. "We'll go somewhere tropical."

"Promise?"

"Sure." But it was far from promising.

The annoying thud from his phone vibrating on the night stand interjects into our tender moment and he exhales.

"Who's calling you at this hour?" I ask as he reaches for it.

I catch the name Alex as he gets out of the bed. "I'll be right back," he says before answering the phone. "Hold on," he tells the stranger on the other end as he puts on a pair of shorts.

Either my imagination is really running rampant this time or I truly just heard a woman reply to him.

My heart is screaming in my ear as I watch him exit the room. My hands begin to shake and I sit up, pulling the covers over my chest, waiting intently for him to come back and calm my worried thoughts.

Thankfully, I don't have to wait too long and within a few minutes he comes back in. But I can immediately tell he's not in a good mood.

"Who was that?" I ask.

"Alex," he sighs. "There's a mix up with some of the steel." His tone is dull, losing all the tenderness it just had.

He gets back into the bed and lies on his back with an arm behind his head. I scoot up beside him and try putting my head back on his chest.

He groans. "I'm not in the mood, Riley."

My face falls and I frown. "Can I try to make it better? I have a really good way I can help." I trace my hand down his stomach.

He stops me from dipping under his waistline. His eyes are empty and careless, almost disgusted when he glares at me.

"You can't just do that to me," I exclaim despairingly. "Make love to me, promise the world, and then shut me out."

"Go to bed, Ri," he says exasperatedly.

"How do you switch so easily?" I plea, fighting the hurt in my throat.

But it's a question left unanswered as he turns over presenting his back to me. I stare at him in disbelief before scowling and wrenching my body onto its side. I curl up, gripping my pillow tight and slamming my eyes shut to prevent the tears. My pulse is ferocious and my body is shaking from anger.

It's long after his breathing levels out and his slight snore begins before I feel the angered rage slip away, allowing me to finally fall asleep all while my mind races all the way to the finish line.

Chapter 11

It's been two days since Brian pulled his Jekyll and Hyde move, and not a damn thing has gotten any better. He's back to the same old fucked up Brian—distant with few words and the least amount of eye contact possible. He's disconnected from us again. And I'm back to feeling inconsequential.

I warn April when she places her chair down that I'm not in a good mood. I don't want to be bothered. I don't want a pick-me-up. I want to sulk and drown in my damn misery today. Thankfully she heeds my warning and respects my wishes, pulling out her phone.

The breeze blows over the blades of grass, bending them one direction only for them to lazily stand back up and wait for another gust to repeat its process. Resilient...those blades are. Even after being knocked down, they stand back up. After being stepped on, they rise back tall. The sun peeks in and out from behind the thick clouds causing the area to brighten and dim.

"Should I tell him you're not in the mood?" April asks amusingly, glancing behind me.

"What?" I turn and follow her eyes to Trenton walking toward us. Instead of groaning because company is the last damn thing I want or rolling my eyes in protest...I smile.

"Hey," Trenton grins. "How are you ladies?"

"Hopefully better now that you're here," April states and I cringe.

He looks between us perplexed but laughs it off. "Glad to be of assistance. But per my students, I'm a downer. I gave them a pop quiz."

"Oh, you're mean," April facetiously breathes out. "You're a monster." Her award-winning act causes me to giggle, and she reaches out and smacks my arm. "Not only does she smile, she laughs too."

This time I roll my eyes.

Trenton drops beside us on the bleachers and it may be my splendid bubbly mood but his relaxed demeanor pisses me off.

"Were you intentionally trying to be a dickhead to Brian or are you just that much of an asshole?" I snap.

The corner of his lips tick, but they never raise into a smile. His expression remains stoic. "I wasn't being a dickhead." And his tone sounds casual.

I narrow my eyes. "Really? 'Cause that's not how I perceived it."

"Riley..." April quietly tries scolding me but I ignore it.

He looks to her and then back to me. "Maybe you read into it wrong?"

I shake my head. "I'm not stupid."

"Didn't say you were," he states.

"Brian reamed her a new ass," April says.

I jerk my head to her. "What business is it of yours?"

She shakes her foot, leaning back in the chair victoriously.

"Really?" Trenton asks with concern. "What'd he say?"

I snap back to him. "I wasn't the only one thinking you were being a smartass."

He spreads his hands. "I'll watch my mouth next time. I'm sorry." But by his tone, he isn't sorry. He's pleased.

I shove my palms into my forehead. "I'm so ready for today to be over."

Open House

"I'm going to head off. Let you simmer down," Trenton says. I catch the ass end of an expression he shares with April, but his smile was sexy and knowing.

"What the fuck was that?" April scolds.

I don't answer.

"What's wrong with you today? Brian on a rampage again?"

I sigh. "What was that look between you and Trenton?"

An innocent cockiness launches across her smirk. "Panty bursting. He knew exactly what he was doing. He's dangerous in a sexy as hell way."

"I swear he's doing this on purpose."

"Doing what?" she ponders.

I drop my hands into my lap frustrated. "The looks. The pop ups. The way he says shit. All of it."

"What if that is just him? What if that *is* his personality? You're not giving the man a break."

I look at her coldly. "Does it help to pretend you don't see anything?"

"You need a stiff fucking drink today," she bites. "This is ridiculous."

"I love you. Just let me stew in peace," I say with my view on my knees.

"Not a problem. I'm here if you need me."

I don't speak to her again until we say our goodbyes, and mine comes with an apology. She kisses my cheek and gifts me an accepting smile, but she doesn't say anything else. That's the wondrous thing about our friendship—we get each other. I'm having an off day and she understands it.

It's after ten when Brian walks through the door and heads straight to the shower without even acknowledging me. Promptly, my blood boils and I barge into the bathroom.

"Hi, honey. How was your day?" I snap sardonically.

He pulls his head out of the spray and wipes the water from his eyes. "Good. Yours?"

"Good."

He tucks his head back behind the glass shower door and I watch him lather the soap and begin washing himself. "What's for dinner?"

"Cold remnants in the microwave," I clip.

I hear his long exhale. "What's wrong?"

I roll my eyes and without a hint of their grand appearance, tears begin to well. Embarrassed by my weakness, I rush out and cry.

By the time he comes out of the bathroom, I've calmed down and am sitting on the side of my bed staring at the lines in the hardwood floors.

"What's wrong?" he asks without any emotion behind it.

I huff a laugh. "I'm tired. Long day." I lie.

And as he always has, he accepts the answer and leaves the bedroom.

It takes all I have to control the rage I feel vibrating throughout me. I want to scream at him, throw things around, and tell him how much I can't stand him right now, but instead, I take a long shaky, calming breath and curl up in the bed.

Chapter 12

Unhappy. The dictionary states a simple, yet powerful definition of the word—not happy. Some of the synonyms that follow suit are sad, sorrowful, dejected, heartbroken, and miserable. It's hard to describe heartache. Everyone is different, experiencing different things. But we all suffer with one thing in common—pain.

Somewhere Brian has vanished. Swallowed whole by the sufferings of work...life somewhere outside of the house. I'm no longer his comfort regardless of how much I do for him. My smile is robotic, forced by love, broken by agony. It's been months of him missing from the dinner table. His smile doesn't light up the room. There isn't time together as a family. And even if his body is physically lying in the bed, he still isn't there.

Our conversations are only as long as a breath holds. We're more roommates now than we've ever been. Intimacy is only in my dreams, reminiscing of the days we once were so madly in love with one another that nothing could separate us. Time has chosen to change us, derail the life we both dreamed of making. Work has played the biggest factor. He used to come home and tell me about his day—the screw ups, the fun times, and of course the bad days. Those conversations have long since ended. I came to grips...I fabricated the illusion he loves me so much he doesn't want to drown me in his own personal hell despite the fact I'm willing to hold his hand through the flames.

Sex has become more of a duty, a chore for both of us. It's passionless. Unromantic. Lacking love. I feel obligated to lie there and enjoy the moments he gives me, but that in itself makes me feel like an underpaid prostitute despite having a home given to me by my suitor.

I'm beginning to resemble Brian—an empty shell.

Over the course of a few weeks, soccer practices and games have become my haven. Between April and Trenton, I look forward to them. They rip me from the personal hell I live in and grant me life, even if it's only for a little bit of time.

"I'm having a cookout at my house this weekend. You coming?" April asks shoving her sunglasses on top of her hair.

I giggle. "And why am I just hearing of this? I could've helped you plan it." Not to mention it'd give me something to focus on.

"Impromptu. Adults only. Jeff will have Josh. I figured it was time to have a blowout since it's been awhile."

"I'll be there," I tell her.

She nods her head. "You too, Mr. B."

Even with him insisting on her calling him by his first name, she refuses.

He pulls his attention from the field. "What do I need to bring?"

"BYOB," she informs him. "And if you want to bring someone, you can. Just one rule. No sex in my house."

He laughs shaking his head. "As sadistic as you are, I'm sure you'd scalp my...nether region and hang them up for a trophy."

She glares while pointing at him. "You best remember that." She smiles and shifts her gaze to me. "Will Brian be joining us?"

I shrug. "I'll ask. I never know his schedule anymore."

She gives me a sad smile and throws the strap of her chair over her shoulder. "Don't worry about food. I've got that taken care of. Will you give me a hand around six?"

I nod, gathering my stuff.

"Great. Party starts at seven."

We all say goodbye and Trenton follows suit as April and I collect our children, praising them for a job well done.

For the first time in over a week, Brian makes it home just as we sit down for dinner.

I smile up to him. "Hey. Hope you're hungry. I made your favorite meal."

He eyes me suspiciously. "What for?"

I dismiss the lack of enthusiasm. "Because I felt like it. You've worked really hard this week."

"I work hard every week," he reminds me.

"I know. I just wanted to do something nice."

"Thanks," he says pulling a beer out of the fridge.

He doesn't give Lucas the same attitude he gives me. Their conversation is fun and of course about soccer. It's the very subject that keeps them bonded together. Lucas tells him a few random things that happened at school or something about an assignment, but somehow it always turns back to soccer.

"April is having her annual party this weekend," I say pushing around my mashed potatoes.

"I won't be able to make it," he says and my heart breaks.

"Why not?" I ask.

He lowers his head and scowls from under his lashes. "Work."

"But it's the weekend and we always have fun when we go."

"Doesn't stop work." He doesn't even look at me when he says it.

I stare at him in disbelief. I've lost my appetite and drop my hands in my lap.

The air has shifted. It's uncomfortable, awkward, intense and thick. Lucas must feel it too because he's quit speaking, occasionally shifting his view between his father and me. I can only imagine what his poor thoughts are. I try offering him a warm smile, but I know it's come off as a sad one instead.

Something about the way Brian just took a swallow from his beer pisses me off. My blood screams and my frustration shatters.

I snap.

"I'm getting sick of this." I level my view on Brian. "You're the damn boss. Take off work and be with me."

He smirks smugly and twirls his fork, rolling his eyes. The darkened glare, the angry creases across his forehead tell me all I need to know about his thoughts.

I shove to my feet, sliding the chair back with my legs, and slam my fist on the table. "Make some fucking time for us, Brian," I scathe.

He raises his brow and the smug smirk transforms into arrogance. He tips his head to Lucas. "Language."

I don't remove my vicious glower.

He drops his fork to the plate with a loud clang and slides his chair back. "I can't." He crosses his arms. "This job has a deadline and I have to meet it."

"A few hours in the evening *of a weekend* can't *possibly* hurt you *that* badly."

"I'm finished with this conversation." He jerks to his feet and starts walking away.

"No you're not!" I yell after him and then twist to Lucas. "I'm sorry, sweetie."

"I hate this," he says.

"I'm sorry," I repeat. "Go play Xbox for a bit."

"Code for you two arguing. I get it."

I puff a heartbroken sigh. "Things will get better."

He scrapes the remnants of food into the trash and then places his plate into the sink. "Can I ride my bike to Josh's?"

I look at him like he just struck gold. "Just be back in an hour."

I wait for him to track out the door before stomping my way over to Brian in the recliner. I snatch the remote, turn off the TV, and hurl it across the room. "Talk to me!"

I'm fuming. The sound of my pulse hammers in my ears.

He sighs, dragging his hands over his face. "About what?"

"This! Us! What the hell is going on, Brian?"

"Riley, I've had a long day. Don't—"

"You always have long days. You're always at work. What about me? What about Lucas? Where do we fit in anymore?"

"What about y'all?" he yells. "You think you're the only one affected by this? Are you that selfish?"

"Don't you dare try turning this on me. Unless you consider me wanting you to spend time with your family or show me a drop of affection selfish, I'm far from it."

Rage drenches the sweat across his forehead and he leaps from the chair, shoving his face into mine. "I put forth the fucking effort. I'm the one keeping this fucking family up."

I push him away from me. "The same excuse you always have but you never do a damn thing different to fix it. Do you even care?"

"If you'd keep your mouth shut and be the little fucking housewife you're supposed to be, life would be much better."

Murder ignites in my glare. "I'm not taking the blame for what's happening between us. *I'm* the one putting in effort. I'm the one keeping your household up. Your little fucking housewife is the only damn thing keeping the house together. *Our* life would be easier if you'd put forth some effort."

"I do!" he roars.

"You don't!" I scream back.

"Do you not think I miss you too?"

"How the hell would I know? You don't even look at me. We don't speak to each other." I choke back a sob, determined to keep my tears at bay. "You promised me. You promised you'd try. You promised things would get better," I plea.

"Quit throwing shit in my face," he barks.

"What? You don't like hearing the promises you've broken?"

He narrows his eyes and I mirror the look.

"You're not you. We're not us. And *you've* made it that way. You used to love loving me. You were always unable to keep your hands off me. We used to laugh. What's changed? Has work destroyed you that badly? Get rid of it!"

Something blasts in his eyes and he turns, slamming his fist into the wall. His chest is rising and falling fiercely, and he doesn't look back as he exits the room.

I don't chase after him. I'm rooted, staring at the dented hole in the wall with my hand over my mouth.

He returns, stomping toward me. His fists are balled at his sides, face red and contorted with madness, his head tilted down glowering with the devil in the reflection of them. I gulp air, backing up so quickly that my back slams against the wall.

His eyes are violently wild, all things resembling Brian absent as he snatches my chin. "What do you want, Riley?" I don't recognize the voice as he slides his other hand down my ribs and squeezes my sex. "You want some fucking attention? Like this? Angry sex. We've never done that." His whisper ends with an audacious growl.

"Stop," I snap, trying to swat him off me.

He squeezes my chin harder, pushing my head against the wall. "Is this what you wanted? Some fucking attention. You have it." His breath is hot, splashing across my cheek as he nips the skin. "Do you want me to come home and fuck you after a long day's work? I'll make you my dirty little housewife."

I manage to get my arm past his and slap him. He releases his grip just enough for me to slide down the wall and out of the raging enclosure of his arms. "What the fuck is wrong with you?" I shout through my fear. I'm scared out of my wits, unsure what the hell has possessed him.

He twists toward me, blinking the rage out of his eyes.

"What the fuck? Stop!" I scream, thunder roaring from my throat. Using every ounce of my strength to get the words out from the top of my lungs, I stomp squeezing my fists at my side.

I run out of the room crying and grab my purse, rushing out the door to my car. Even though he isn't pursuing, I can't get out of there fast enough. I screech my tires lurching out of the driveway, scrambling to get to April's.

I'm a sobbing mess pulling into her driveway. My body is shaking from the sheer amount of livid adrenaline scorching my veins and I'm barely able to walk to her door. I'm gasping for air, bawling when she answers the door.

With one look, she rushes me to her bedroom, pushing the door shut behind us. "What happened?" She wraps her arms around my shoulders.

I can't answer. I can't breathe. I squeeze her, weeping on her shoulder.

"Riley? What happened?" she repeats.

I swallow, trying to compose myself. "We've never had this bad of an argument."

She wipes my hair off my face. "Did he hit you?"

I shake my head but the images of his icy, dead eyes staring back at me haunt me. I lose it and sob harder.

I don't know how long we've sat here, but I'm gassed out with nothing else to give. My chest hurts from the sobs that have wracked my body. My face is sticky from the salty tears. I push off the bed, go to the bathroom and splash my face with cold water in hopes of settling the puffiness under my eyes.

April appears at the door and I look to her worried eyes in the mirror. "I'm okay."

"You sure?" she asks.

I nod.

"Do you want something to drink?" Her sympathetic brown eyes are drowning with sadness.

"I've got to get Lucas home."

"He's more than welcome to spend the night."

"He's got school tomorrow," I tell her.

Her lips pull into a tender smile. "As does my son."

"Thanks, but we'll be okay."

"I'm here if you need me," she says quietly.

I hug her and pull myself together.

After Lucas puts his bike in her garage, we don't exchange any words during the ride home. The pain and raw emotions in the air are so thick they take my breath away. The extreme heaviness sits on my chest. And I can almost swear it's affecting Lucas the same way.

I'm assuming Brian went to bed because he hasn't come downstairs since we've been home, and I'm not setting foot in the bedroom. I kiss Lucas goodnight and make my way back to the living room. The couch is my small version of my king-sized bed. It will be my safe haven for the night.

Chapter 13

Brian has made it his personal commitment to steer clear from us both. He leaves before Lucas or I wake, and he's home after we've gone to bed. I haven't slept in the bed. I won't. The man who sleeps there is a stranger and I'm not lying beside him. We haven't talked since our big argument. Actually, I've only seen him once and that was out of the crack of my pretend-sleeping eyes.

Since Josh is with his dad, Lucas decided to spend the night with his friend Craig. He's a sweet kid with an even sweeter mother who absolutely adores Lucas.

I drop him off and head to April's to give her a hand with setting everything up for the party.

"Don't you look good," she chirps opening the door.

I decided tonight I needed to do something for me, something to make me feel better about myself, and what better way than to play dress up. I threw on my favorite pair of jeans with rips and tears up the legs with a dark orange spaghetti strap tank top and a pair of black, strappy high heel sandals. I feel gorgeous.

"Thanks." I close the door behind me.

I place plate after plate of finger foods onto the longest table that we set up along the back wall of her living room. There's got to be at least a mile of breads, meats, vegetables and fruits. When she goes all out, she does so in fashion. I move outside and plug in the white lights draping around her dark-stained Messina gazebo and tie back its sheer curtains hanging beautifully from the corners. It's my favorite spot of her house.

People begin to trickle in—some I know, others are new faces, and the rest are people I've seen only at her annual parties. As April mingles, bouncing from person to person, I put on my party face and blend into the crowd. There's such a variety of people, ranging from the incredibly snobbish—how dare she not serve us lobster on gold plates—from her work to the people who fall perfectly in the middle—happy to be here, smiling and enjoying their time.

I need a breather from the crowd, so I make my way out of her French doors and onto the dark wicker couch under the dimly lit Messina with my glass of wine. I'm the only one out here and I'm grateful for it because thoughts of Brian are beginning to crowd my mind. Helping me push them aside, I inhale a long breath of the night air and watch the clouds push through the moonlight, causing a purple haze of mysteriousness.

"What are you so deeply thinking about?" Trenton's voice startles me and I jump just a little.

He smiles with a beer in his hand, and I pull my legs up, giving him a spot to sit at the opposite end of the couch. Under the soft golden lights, the lighter tones in his hair seem brighter. And as weird as it sounds, seeing him dressed differently in a seafoam green shirt, tight and showing off his athletic build, with dark faded jeans and chukka boots instead of slacks, seems to make him look better. I guess it's because he looks more relaxed than what he wears at school.

"Hey," I say. "It got crowded fast and I ran out of air."

"How many people did she invite?" He laughs.

"I've told her she needs to rent out a hotel floor." I giggle but it fades off as I look back to the night sky.

"What's on your mind?"

Slowly, I blink back to him and give him a weak smile. "Nothing."

"Ah. The infamous nothing. Must be something pretty major then."

"Why can't it ever just be nothing?"

"Do women ever stop thinking?"

I tip my glass toward him. "Good point."

He lets silence gather around us. It isn't awkward, nor does it feel uncomfortable. Just his presence gives me comfort in my dismal thinking, and knowing I'm not alone in this gloomy night lifts my spirits a bit.

"Do men really have such bad days they shut out everything they love?" I ask into the night air, not looking to him. "I'm not talking about one or two bad days. I mean months or more."

Out of the corner of my eye, I see him tilt his head to the side looking out to April's manicured yard. "I've never had them. I'd suppose a day here or there would make sense, but not months. At some point, I'd say you'd begin to see the destruction it's causing."

"Hmph," I grunt.

"How long's it been?"

I take a slow sip of the sweet white wine and glance to him, pushing my lips tight. "Is it sad I can't remember? The worst has reared its ugly head in the past six months."

"Have you talked to him?"

I laugh under my breath. "Add that to my list, just before begged, cried, and most recently screamed."

"What's his reasoning?"

I pull my legs into my chest, twisting my body to face him. "He blames work and tells me it'll get better after the job. The same excuse I've heard for years now."

"Can I ask you something personal?" his tone holds caution.

"Yeah." I nod.

"Are you still in love with him?"

I can feel the glassiness spread over my eyes as I lose focus on Trenton and the fence behind him comes into the blurry center of my attention. My throat tightens. "No." I shake my head. "I love him, but I'm not in love with him."

"If you're not in love with him, why are you torturing yourself with unhappiness?"

I shrug. "He's all I know. My first love." I smile brokenheartedly. "I guess I'm wishing the pieces would fall back in place."

He shifts toward me and drapes his arm over the back of the couch. "Nothing is ever the same the second go around. Besides, your feelings didn't change overnight."

"I guess I wanted to pretend it was all still there. I wanted to believe we were in some kind of slump. Everyone has had them. I'm no different. It's conflicting, the same man I once was madly in love with..." I trail off.

"What about counseling?" he asks with deep compassion.

"He's too manly for that."

"My uneducated guess is neither one of you are in love with each other anymore and are too scared to admit it. It's not a bad thing. It's life. People change. Sometimes as you're growing up, you grow apart."

I smile at him. "For such a young man, you're pretty philosophical."

He laughs. "I'm less than a year younger than you."

"You're basically in diapers," I tease.

He takes a swig of his beer and grants me a cute and playful smile. "I'm going back in. Might as well take advantage of free food since I'm a growing boy. Do you want anything?"

"No. Thank you."

He pats my shoulder. "Don't be afraid of change, Riley. Welcome it. Life has evolved around it."

I stare blankly at the wooden planks of the fence. I'm not afraid of change. I'm petrified of what follows it—the aftermath.

Trenton's words continue to swirl in my mind and I think he's right. I want counseling and I pray Brian will agree to it because I know we love each other so deeply that we don't want to lose it. Nothing but good can come from getting professional help, from getting an outsider's view.

Tired of thinking about something so forlorn, I make my way back inside, refill my glass and find April. I stand quietly beside her, listening to the group of women talk about some of the HOA rules and regulations, which makes me thank my lucky stars we don't have one. Even though we live a few roads away and share the same sidewalk, I don't have to answer to the apparent asshole leaders of the organization.

A sensation trickles down the back of my neck and I scan the room to see Trenton eyeing me from the other side in a group of all men. It's a unique stare—full of wonder, worry, compassion, and thought. It provokes me to give a small grin and he matches mine, raising his beer to a silent "cheers."

Another hour and once again, I've had my fill of people. I've come to the conclusion I'm a soccer mom with no life. I don't know half of what they're talking about. I'm unable to add to the conversations and they never steer toward my expertise of motherhood.

April has a koi fish pond in the far corner of her back yard surrounded by tall leafy bushes. It's small, beautiful and tranquil. The sound of water trickling, spilling into the pond brings serenity. The moonlight dances on the moving water, glinting and animating the ripples. It's very soothing.

"Why do I constantly find you outside alone?" Trenton asks.

Thing is...I felt him before he spoke. A weird tug in my chest alerted me to his presence. "Why do you always know where to find me when I hide from the crowd?"

"It's a knack." He chuckles.

"You'd be a bastard to play hide and seek with," I snort. "Could it be the fact every time I look up, you're watching me?" I give him a shit-eating grin.

His lips twitch. "Someone has to keep an eye on you."

I hum. "Nice to know someone does."

"That's what friends are for, right?" There's an emptiness to his tone.

"I don't see how April does this yearly. There's way too many people in there for me."

He takes a swallow from his beer and we both settle into a quietness, watching and listening to the water spill into the little pond.

"It's beautiful. Don't you think?"

"Very." His husky tone pulls me to look over at him gazing at me.

My brows pinch together. "Do what?"

He licks his lips and shakes his head. "Fuck it," he mumbles, dropping his beer in the grass and walking me backward against the fence.

He places his elbow on the wood, lowering himself to my face. His body doesn't touch mine, but I can feel the intensity.

"Please don't do this to me," I whisper with a shaky voice.

His lustful eyes flick from my lips to my eyes. "I want to kiss you, Riley."

"I'm...I—"

"Taken?" he finishes my fumbling sentence. "I can be the man you've dreamed of."

I swallow hard, resisting the urge to give in. I'd be lying if I said I haven't fantasized about his lips against mine. "Please don't." He leans closer, dissipating some of the space distancing our lips. "Please don't make me do something I'd regret."

"It wouldn't be a regret."

"I'm not a cheater," I tell him.

"He doesn't love you," he says.

"Neither do you," I reply.

"I could if you'd let me."

I shake my head. "I can't."

"Because you've never let yourself. Let yourself feel it. I wouldn't ever let you fall out of love with me. I wouldn't leave you to hurt like you are."

"You don't know that," I say.

"Dammit, Riley, I want you," he whispers, his hazel eyes roaming my face. "I can make you happy. Bring out the gorgeous smile of yours. A woman like you should be appreciated, respected, and loved to the fullest. You'd be my queen—"

"I don't think we should see each other again," I choke out, interrupting him.

Hurt dawns in his expression and he exhales a frustrated sigh. "As much as it rips my heart out of my chest, I agree. You're torture for me."

His gaze darts between my eyes and lips before they settle with yearning and he takes a step away, allowing relief to sink in. Our stares linger. Emotions are drenching his expression and in this very moment, I see how much he truly cares for me.

He picks up his beer bottle and takes one last look back—angst and defeat—and then he's gone.

I gulp in air, leaning back on the wooden fence, and drag my hands over my face. "Holy shit..." I sigh.

I knew there was an attraction between us, chemistry even, but I didn't know he felt so deeply. Confusion settles a fog in my thoughts and I muster up the strength to go inside and excuse myself...risking the uncomfortable encounter with him.

April's too busy entertaining to see my distress when I slide up beside her and tell her I'm heading out. Thankfully, I paused a conversation she was interested in, which made our goodbye much quicker. I'm incredibly relieved I don't see Trenton as I rush out of April's house. Half of me is scared to see him, in fear of how uncomfortable it will all be now knowing exactly how he feels. I often thought it. Now, he solidified it.

Chapter 14

I park beside Brian's SUV and lean my head against the head rest taking a few steady breaths to relieve my nerves. When I finally make my way in, Brian is at the island with a beer in front of him. As he lifts his head, I can immediately tell he's drunk—his black hair is messy and his eyes are glassy.

"How was the party?" he asks with a slight slur.

"Good. As usual, she invited a lot of people. I missed you. I wished I had your arm." I smile tenderly. I always felt the safest, the sexiest, and the most prideful when I was by his side with my arm weaved into his.

He licks his lips and frowns. "Don't start."

"I'm not," I say somberly.

I step out of my heels and bend picking them up.

"I want you to leave," he says and I jerk straight up.

"Do what?"

He drops his hand heavily on the counter. "You heard me right. I want you to leave," he repeats.

I flinch at the laceration his words cause and immediately the vision of him becomes blurry through my tears. "You don't mean that. You're drunk."

He shakes his head. "I do. I do mean it, Riley." His face sets into a hardened stare. "I'm done. We've been done. No use to keep on. Get out." The emptiness of his words shatter my soul.

"No," I state matter-of-factly. "You don't mean it. You've been drinking."

He takes a frustrated breath. "I'm not going to argue about this. Drinking or not, I've made my decision. Now, get the hell out."

I swallow the lump in my throat, staring at him. He doesn't budge, piercing me with cold eyes. Somehow, I find the strength to pull my shoulders back and wipe the tears off my cheeks.

"Thanks for fighting just as hard as I did," I snap angrily. I snatch my purse off the counter and stomp out of the house, slamming the door behind me.

Anger controls me right now. My outrage isn't letting the hurt emerge as it should. Instead of bawling from a broken heart, I'm beyond pissed. Fuck him for giving up after I've fought so hard. Screw him for waiting until I hurt so badly to give me a glimpse of how he was feeling months after me begging and pleading for us to rekindle everything. He promised we'd be okay. He fucking promised me.

I drive back to the only place I know to go, the one with all the damn people still crowding the house.

I find April and tug her elbow. "I need to talk to you," I grit.

Comprehension dawns in her expression and she moves us from the middle of the crowd back to her bedroom, where nights before I cried over Brian and me arguing.

"He's done. Kicked me out of the house," I shout the moment the door clicks, throwing my purse down on her bed.

Her brown eyes widen with confusion. "He did what? Why?"

I throw my hands up. "He didn't give me a reason. Told me he was done."

"That's all he gave you?"

"Yup. That's all he fucking gave me. Eleven years and I'm out on my ass in a blink of an eye. No warnings. No hints. Nothing."

Sympathy. It's a look I've never been able to handle well. I've never liked to be the reason, but her expression, her sad eyes...the realness, and then the truth dawns on me. "Oh my God, Lucas." I suck in air and my anger melts away to sorrow. I drop my face into my hands. "He's...How..."

"You two can stay here until you get on your feet. You stay in the guest room. Lucas can bunk with Josh. They'll love it. I'll see what I can do about getting you a job. Take a deep breath. This will all be okay."

"How could he?" I say, knowing full well I saw all this coming. "How could he just up and kick me out without a notice?"

Her lips contort into a frown, unable to answer my question. "I've got to get back out there." She points to the door. "Do you need anything? Care to join me?"

"No. I'm going to hide in the guest bedroom. Is Trenton still here?" I ask.

"I haven't seen him in a while. Don't do anything brash, Riley."

I shake my head. "Nothing like that. He's the last person I want to see right now."

Her eyes soften. "I'll check on you in a bit, but if you need me before come get me. Okay?"

I offer a weak smile.

She hugs my neck. "I promise this will be okay."

I didn't sleep well in the empty, cold guest bed. The room didn't feel familiar. All the scents were foreign, and for the first time, I missed hearing Brian's light snore. I wept holding a pillow and ended up crying myself to sleep. Throughout the night, I woke up many times, rolling over to see if Brian was there and this was all a bad dream. Unfortunately, Brian wasn't there and reality was heartless.

I lie here, staring at the ceiling and taking in my surroundings. This is my new home until I find myself another one. I hear movement coming from the kitchen and I make my way toward it. April is in her purple fluffy robe, pouring herself a cup of coffee when she sees me and grabs another mug.

"How are you holding up?" she asks handing me the cup.

"I don't know," I answer honestly. "I feel numb."

The first sip of coffee is bright and tangy, waking up my taste buds and warming my dry throat. "I'm going to call him. Lucas needs his stuff for school and I need clothes." I exhale a long breath. "Can I take the coffee into the room?"

She furrows her brows giving me a ridiculous look. "That's your part of the house. You make a mess, you clean it up."

I smile, making my way past her and back down the long hall. I grab my cell, set my coffee on the nightstand and sit on the side of the bed.

It only rings twice when a tired voice answers.

"Did I wake you?" I ask.

"Yeah."

"I'm sorry." But honestly I'm not.

"It's fine," he grumbles, sounding as if he's sitting up.

"Is this real?" My voice exits in a dense and unfamiliar tone.

"Yeah, Riley, it is," he sighs.

I clear the lump out of my throat. "I need to come get a few things for me and Lucas."

"Send April. I'll have some of your stuff ready."

"I can't come and get it?" I ask defensively. "It's my house too!" Or it was.

"This is hard enough. Don't make it any harder."

"If you feel that way, why aren't we trying to make it work? Counseling? Something. I'm willing to try. It doesn't have to be this way," I plea.

He takes a shaky breath. "Pull half of the savings. It's yours. You can come get your things when I'm not home. I trust you."

"What about Lucas? What am I supposed to tell him?" I'm losing control over my emotions.

"The truth. We fell apart, Riley. For years, I've been miserable at work and taking it out on you. I don't spend nearly enough time with Lucas and I don't care enough to spend time with you. None of us deserve the unhappiness. Lucas doesn't deserve parents who constantly fight."

I scoot against the headboard and pull a pillow to my chest. "And what if he wants to see you?"

"I'll always be a phone call away. I can have him every other weekend and then some days after school during the week. If I'm working late on those days, I'll let him know."

Tears sting my eyes and I softly cry. "Brian..."

"This isn't easy for me either."

"Sounds like you've planned it all out," I say curtly knowing he's thought this out without talking to me.

"I did."

The bite of his words burn my skin.

"I'm tired of fighting and both of us hurting. I loathe coming home to the pissed off eyes and bitter tones, and I hate that I don't care enough to change it. Send April when she has time. I'll gather everything you need for the night. Tomorrow while I'm at work, gather your things."

He hangs up.

He fucking hangs up.

I stare at my phone in disbelief. He doesn't care enough to change it. Maybe that was the fundamental shift that happened to our relationship years ago—he quit caring.

I grip my warm cup and pad back down the hallway. April is sitting at the table, staring mindlessly out the window into her backyard.

"I need to ask you a favor," I say sitting across from her. "Brian doesn't want me to come and get anything today but he said he'd gather a few things for Lucas and me if you go and get it. Do you have time today to run by and grab it?"

She blinks up to me. Her lip curls in disgust and she sits back. "He's being a dick, huh?" She shakes her head. "Yeah. I can."

"I need to go get Lucas. Brian said he'll have everything ready."

She nods her head toward the bathroom. "There's an extra toothbrush still in the package under the sink. You can change into something of mine if you'd like. Yoga pants are in the bottom drawer of my dresser. Trust me. They make everything better." Her smile is laced with a sadness that has me choking back tears.

"I feel like I've been robbed. A victim of a crime. Everything is in limbo and my emotions aren't making sense," I admit.

"Do they ever? And who's to say your feelings are supposed to make sense?"

"I don't know. I think I may be in shock. I'm not devastated like I thought I would be, but I'm not happy about it either."

"Maybe you've been ready for this more than you knew?"

I leave her question unanswered.

I brush my teeth and make my way into her bedroom, grabbing a loose pink blouse and leaving my jeans on. There's a soft knock on the door before April calls out to tell me she's grabbing Josh and getting my things.

I'm heavy with woe—troubled at the plateaued feelings. I'm sad and feeling a bit guilty because I have a sense of relief, but I also feel like a failure.

My feet seem to know what to do—one step in front of the other—as I make my way to my car. Everything seems hazy, outlined in a thick fog as I crank my car and immediately shut off the radio. We all know how the universe enjoys purposely lining things up. I'm sure the radio will play every sad, heartbreaking song one after another from the 1950s to now.

I call Barbara, Craig's mother, and tell her I'm not feeling well so she can just send Lucas out when I get there. Thankfully, she doesn't press the issue and agrees. Then right on cue as I pull up, my scruffy blond-haired boy comes bounding out the front door. My chest swells with hurt, knowing the conversation I'll soon be having with him.

"Hey, Mom," he says jumping into the back seat.

"Hey, sweetie. How was your night?"

"We swam all night. Barb turned the lights on in the pool and they changed colors. Red looked sic. It made it look like we were swimming in blood."

"Well, that sounds like it was...fun?" I laugh.

"It was so cool. And I had sausage, pancakes, and biscuits this morning," he adds.

"Pancakes and biscuits?" I chuckle.

"I put syrup on my biscuit. Tasted like a dry pancake."

I laugh at his description. "I'm glad you had a good time. Hey, we're going to hang with April for a bit."

"Is Josh there?" he rushes out in excitement.

"She went to get him."

"Good. I can't wait to tell him about Craig's pool."

During the rest of the drive, he tells me about his dives from the diving board—most of them ending in belly flops. From there it turned into a belly flop competition with who could make the best sounding one. I wince as he explains that after his third or fourth one, it brought tears to his eyes automatically deeming Craig the winner. He gushes about how they slept in the basement and how it's set up like an apartment "straight from New York City." And finally, how he tried getting Craig to watch a scary movie, but Craig ended up chickening out on him.

He's still rambling on as we pull into April's and is still going over every single detail as I unlock the door. It isn't five minutes later when April comes through the door with Josh talking her ear off. He pauses when he sees us sitting on the couch and then makes a beeline to Lucas.

Lucas eyes his book bag suspiciously as April sets both bags down.

"Follow me, kiddo. I gotta talk to you," I say.

My pulse has never been so loud as I walk him down the hall to "my" bedroom. I feel like I'm about to jump out of a plane.

I take a seat beside him on the bed and pat his leg. "I don't really know where to start." I clear my throat. "Dad and I have decided it's best if we go our separate ways."

I want to puke.

"Like break up?" He flicks his surprised eyes to me.

"Yeah, baby, like break up." I fight back my cry, swallowing through a tight throat. "You and I are going to stay here until I can get us our own place. If it's okay with you, you'll bunk with Josh. Dad said he'll get you every other weekend and possibly some through the week for a few hours."

He twists his thumbs. "Mom? Are you okay?"

Tears sting my eyes. "Yeah, baby, I'm okay."

"You two fought a lot," he tells me.

"I know," I sigh. "I'm really sorry about that."

"Is it okay that I'm sad?"

I pull him in for a hug. "Yes. We're all sad, but we know it's better for all of us if we live apart instead of living together unhappy."

He looks up to me. "Is it okay that I'm happy too?"

I puff a laugh. "Yes, baby. It's okay."

"Mom?"

"Yeah?"

"Could you quit calling me baby? I'm ten. I'm not a baby anymore."

I kiss the top of his head. "You'll be my baby until the day I'm no longer needed on Earth. But yes, kiddo, I'll quit calling you baby."

"It's totally not cool. Craig's mom calls him Craigo. I don't think Lucas-o sounds good. We need to find something cooler than kiddo."

I take the back of my fingers to his cheek. "Are you sure you're okay with all of this?"

He shrugs. "It sucks. I'm gonna miss Dad, but you said it will make everyone happy. You're always right and I want everyone happy, too."

My soul swells from his sweet innocence, and I'm struggling to fight off the tears now. "Go get settled in Josh's room. I'll be there in a minute."

As he leaves the room, I try my damnedest to steady my emotions by taking slow breaths—in through my nose, out through my mouth. I need to be strong, if not for me, for him.

Chapter 15

It's been two months since Brian and I split up. April was able to get me a job working in one of the retail stores the same week I moved in with her. And next week, I've got an interview within the company for an HR assistant position. It's been years since I've worked and adjusting to it was difficult, but I thoroughly enjoy it. I also received a jolting reminder of why I loathed working with the public when I was younger. Now grown, my feelings on the matter haven't changed.

April divulged a deeply hidden secret one night over wine. Really long story short, she had gotten a friend to purchase a house while she and Jeff were going through the divorce, just in case. Afterward, she got the house put in her name. She admitted she kept it and didn't sell it because she had a sneaking suspicion I'd need it. At first, it really hurt my feelings knowing she thought Brian and I would one day split, but then, I got it. She was the one I vented to. She was the outsider looking in. So of course, she'd see it coming even if I refused to.

She agreed to rent it to me for just the regular monthly payments until the house is paid off, and then, it would be mine. I agreed and she wrote up a legal document. I'll be an official home owner in a little under two years.

I moved into it about two weeks after he and I split. I spent the first night in eleven years alone in a house I was new to. Everything was unfamiliar, but I felt at home and peaceful. It's adorable—gray siding with dark trim and a cute covered front porch with a back deck. The interior is simple. The living room opens to the kitchen and, because there isn't a dining room, there's an eating area large enough for a small round table in the kitchen. It has three bedrooms with Lucas' room and the guest room across the hall from one another, a full bathroom beside Lucas' room, and the master bedroom at the very end of the hall. The master has an en-suite and I'm excited. For the first time in years, I can make it as girly as I want.

After I pulled half of the savings Brian said I could have, I was officially taken off the bank accounts. That hurt like hell. April borrowed Jeff's truck and went with me to help move my things out of Brian's house. I took everything we decided I could. Lucas' bed, the guest bed, part of the kitchen utensils, and of course, all our clothing. I cried that day. Bawled like a baby as I packed my family into boxes, leaving the man I loved so deeply behind. I took some of the pictures, mainly of Lucas, and left the rest for Brian to deal with. Splitting was his decision. He can deal with the memories in his face.

My ten-year-old son has now become the man of the house, helping me with things I'd normally get Brian to do. He seems to like it because he walks around here with a different confidence level.

For the first month, Brian called Lucas every night and talked to him for ten to twenty minutes, but it didn't last long. Now it has dwindled to two or three times a week, if he's lucky.

Lucas' soccer team never made it to the championships. Unfortunately, they lost their biggest match, but I was surprised how well Lucas handled it. I spotted Trenton that day in the bleachers two over from me, but he never spoke and I never caught him glancing at me. Brian also showed up—late, but he still came just in time to give Lucas a pep talk to brighten his spirits.

Brian and I have remained civil. We went from parents to co-parents. While it's a huge adjustment for him, it's one I was already familiar with. It wasn't like Brian was ever at home. The only difference today holds is the fact I have a job.

The weeks following the move into my new place, I went through many weird emotions. I came out of the numbness with my emotions raw and roaring with an anger I've never experienced before. I was pissed. Raging with anger. And when the confusion set in, it made me even more mad. I couldn't understand why something that used to be so great broke apart and crumbled in my hands. I also had a hard time wrapping my head around all the effort Brian started putting into Lucas. More so than he had ever in over five years. When he first started calling Lucas every night, it would eat me alive because one of my very pleas was for him to call me just to let me know he was running late. It took everything I had not to make a big deal, but I took the high road and contained my annoyance.

April had told me there were stages of emotions in a breakup. I thought she was insane, but looking back, it all makes sense. One evening while she was here, she said I went through them pretty quickly and thought, in my heart, I was ready for this. Honestly, as much as I'm ashamed to admit it, I think I was too. I still love Brian, but he'll never be the same guy I fell in love with. Just like I told Trenton at April's party, I knew I had fallen out of love and I was just holding on for the sake of holding on, pretending everything was okay when I didn't have anything to pretend for. Brian and I were on the same page. We just didn't know it until it was over.

We were both done. I just needed a gentle shove.

Chapter 16

"You sure you're going to be all right?" Lucas asks bringing his bag down the hallway.

Every time he leaves to go to Brian's, he frets about my safety. He's worried since I'm a female alone without him here, something will happen.

"Yes. I'll be fine. Don't worry about me," I tell him kissing him on top of the head.

"If you get scared, sleep with your light on. It helps me."

I laugh. "I scared the boogie monsters out a long time ago. They're more scared of me than I am of them." I hold up a fist. "Trust me."

"Whoa." He holds both hands open. "Remember, you'll never be the evil villain. Your laugh is horrible."

"Hey!" I exclaim with a giggle. "I don't need a hero. I can be one."

"You'll need a hero, Mom. You're a girl."

"What's me being a girl have to do with anything?"

A knock on the door ends our playful banter and sends my heart leaping out of my chest.

I pull open the door, forcing an unreadable expression that I pray isn't giving away my nerves. "Hi."

His wide jaw shifts into a smile, his brown worried eyes change to happiness, and he gives me a once over. "Hey."

I don't budge from the door. I don't want him in my house. He's not allowed. He shut me out and I'm keeping him out.

"You look—"

"Lucas! Dad is ready," I call out interrupting him. "No use for compliments. Don't make this more awkward than it already is," I whisper my strength.

He frowns just before Lucas comes around the door, wrapping his arms around Brian's waist. They embrace for a long moment when Brian finally ends it and tells him to grab his bag.

"I have to work until three Sunday. Do you want me to pick him up or will—"

"I'll bring him back," he rushes out, eyeing me with compassion. "Do you like your job?"

In the past, I loved the look he's giving me right now. I'd melt into his arms knowing how much he cared for me. Mentally, I shake away the memories. "I do. I'm interviewing for a position in the corporate office Monday."

He smiles proudly. "That's good. Good luck."

"Thanks," I say moving out of Lucas' way.

He turns and gives me a big hug. "Remember, you're no hero. Use my bat."

I laugh. "Did you leave it where I can find it?"

"Put it on your bed," he chuckles.

I say my goodbye and then slide back into the house, shutting the door and dropping my head on the black wooden surface. *Nothing is the same the second go around.* I know and as hurtful as it is, I'm done. I'm not going to fall into the web of familiarity just because I'm comfortable in those arms and yearn for the same looks he gave me tonight. I'm not allowing myself to be set up for another heart break, one I know will probably hurt more than the first time around.

I open my eyes and scan my empty house. For the first time in two weeks, I am completely alone—in the quiet, in total peacefulness.

I make a steak salad, one fit for a family of three, and laugh at myself as I try stuffing myself to the gills. But there's no use. I flip through the channels, but there's nothing enticing. So I do what sounds the best—I ready myself for bed.

"Not even thirty years old, and I'm in the bed on a Friday night before nine thirty," I snort to the empty room, pulling my covers back and crawling into bed.

The darkness begins playing tricks on me, so I turn on the TV and mute the sound. Lucas was right. I'm a wimp.

Saturday came and went peacefully and very, very quietly. It felt weird not to make breakfast for Lucas and have our morning chitchats. But it was also freeing. I felt free not having anyone but me to worry about. There wasn't anything to do. No responsibilities. I didn't want to wear a bra, so I didn't as I cleaned the house unsure what the rest of the week held.

But today, I have to get up and be an adult. Unfortunately, I have to do this thing called work.

I'm working the men's department, a section I actually enjoy as much as the children's section. No offense to the women, but snobby never looked good on anyone. Men are composed, reserved, and let's face it, they dislike shopping so much that it's over and done with quickly.

I'm folding pants and putting them on the new display when I feel his presence. Even though he has visited my dreams and holds my daydreams hostage, I haven't seen him since Lucas' last game. I close my eyes and take a second to soak in the magnitude of the sweet intensity, scared to death to turn around.

"When did you start here?" he questions, and I finally turn around to acknowledge him.

In jeans and a loose fitted t-shirt, Trenton is stunning as usual. His hazel eyes gleam more of the green today, and his smile is leery but welcoming.

"I've been here for a month or so." I smile to him.

He grunts. "Proves how little shopping I've done."

I reach for another pair of pants and fold them, placing them neatly on the top of the stack, looking at anything but him.

He doesn't move.

Inwardly, I sigh and glance up to him. "Is there something I can help you with?"

The right side of his lips pull up. "How have you been?"

"Good," I say with pep, leaving out just how crappy I've been in private.

"Lucas says you two moved."

Crap...I tighten my lips. "We did." I pretend to give a damn about the time and look at my watch. "If there isn't anything I can help you with, I need to get going. There's a truck coming in," I lie.

And he knows it. Instead of calling me out with words, his raised brow and sly smirk do the job. "It's good to see you."

"You too." I rush off.

One thing I've learned being apart from Brian is that I miss Trenton's friendship incredibly. I had become emotionally involved with him and gained a friendship I wish we still had. But he crossed a line and now that I know where he wants to be, there isn't a way to be friends. You can't possibly be friends with someone you lust for. It's impossible to keep it strictly platonic.

It's been hours and I can't shake Trenton from my mind. He destroyed my clear, carefree thoughts and the rest of the day, he swirled my mind. I hate myself for allowing it, for not being able to shut it off or distract myself.

On the way home from work, Brian texts me and says he's bringing Lucas home around five—right at dinner time. I want to argue with him and say I know he's doing it on purpose, but there isn't a point to the matter. He doesn't know my schedule even though my routines from when we lived together haven't changed. He wasn't ever home to witness them, so how would he know now?

I shower, throw some makeup on because...well, just because, and start cooking dinner—baked chicken with mashed potatoes and macaroni and cheese, Brian's favorite, because I'm in a spiteful mood.

I'm reaching into the fridge when the front door bursts open and Lucas comes strolling into the house. I abandon everything and rush to him to give him a hug like I haven't seen him in weeks.

"Umm...mom? You're kind of choking me here?" His voice is muffled by my arms.

Quickly, I let loose. "I just..." I pull him right back into my chest. "I missed you so much."

"I was gone two days," he tells me in a laugh.

"What? Am I not allowed to miss you...?" The ending of my question slows when I notice Brian smiling and watching me. I let go of

Lucas. "Thanks for bringing him home." I feel weird for saying that since Lucas' home is his home too.

He glances behind me and then points into the living room. "May I come in?"

Warning bells chime in my head. "No. Maybe another time."

He looks wounded as he shifts on his feet. "Okay. Well, have a good night."

"You too." I shut the door.

Does the uncomfortable feeling ever go away?

Lucas heads to his room to put his things up and quickly jumps in the shower before dinner. You'd think after experiencing the most awkward of awkwardnesses with Brian, my thoughts would be of him, but you'd be wrong. Instead, my head lands right back into Trentonville and for an instant, I wonder if he's thinking of me too.

Lucas slides in his socks across the linoleum floor and into the table just as I turn and place his plate on it.

"Dad took me to the ice skating rink," he says after we say our blessing.

It catches me off guard, but I don't let the hurt simmer to the top. "Did you have fun?"

"I'm a better soccer player than hockey. I can't stay up. Neither can Dad," he titters.

I nod. "Your dad has never been good on the ice. The first time he took me, he bragged like he knew what he was doing. Stayed on his butt more than his feet." I giggle at the memory.

"That's what he said."

"I'm surprised he admitted it. He denied that for years."

He shrugs. "Dad talked about you a lot."

"He did? Like what?" I ask, trying to sound unaffected.

He glances up with a sad look. "I think he misses you.

The statement not only irritates me but devastates me. "Well, we all miss each other," I say nonchalantly. "It's all a big change."

"Did you know Dad was nervous when he asked you out?"

"He texted me out," I correct him.

"He told me he had typed it out days before but was too scared to send it."

This crushes me. "I'm done talking about Dad." I take a sip of my tea, choking down the emotions he unknowingly just ripped open.

Lucas grins widely. "Did you sleep with my bat?"

"I did. It stayed right beside my bed. I'm pleased to report no burglars, boogie monsters, or villains."

"Good." He nods his head.

Since there isn't much he can help me with, Lucas plays Xbox while I clean up the kitchen. I feel like Brian orchestrated a plan and manipulated Lucas by telling him things from our past he's not felt the need to delve into before just because he knew it was going to get back to me. I can't figure out if this was some sort of ploy to win me back. Why would he bring the past up, or better yet, take Lucas to the very place he and I shared some of our best times?

It confuses me to wonder if he truly misses me. Even if he does, do I really care? I'm happier where I'm at now, even if I am alone. At least now I can say I'm not lonely.

Chapter 17

I'm nervous as hell. Panic is knocking in my chest as I'm worried sick I'm going to bomb this interview. It's been more than eleven years since I've had to do this. Even with the retail position, I didn't have an interview. I got the job without even a handshake. But this...this position is big and career promising. This grants me a great job for many years to come and can pave the road to a bright future.

I'm dressed to impress. My chestnut brown hair is down, curving with loose waves. I'm wearing a crimson red blazer skirt suit with a lacy black shirt underneath and black heels. Why? Because the color red exudes a strong and powerful message. Plus, it's energizing and I feel fabulous in it.

I take a deep breath, pull my shoulders back and open the door into the lobby. The receptionist smiles widely when she greets me and leads me down two long halls. Her blonde hair sways back and forth with each step and I can't help but wonder how in the world she's able to walk so steady in heels so high. As she pushes through a wooden door, I inhale the deepest breath I've ever taken, set my smile, and walk in.

The interview couldn't have gone any better. April was there, which made me feel more confident and much more comfortable. They asked many questions, but April knew the questions that would make me shine. She already knew my answers. And when I delivered them, I did so flawlessly. The meeting was only thirty minutes long before they began trading notes and whispering amongst themselves.

Soon after, April stood with a large smile and her hand out for me to shake.

If I could put words into a frame the way they seem to look when they're said, I would mount her words on my wall. "Congratulations. You start Thursday."

It takes all I have not to dance out the door when April tells me the next two days are paid vacation and that I don't need to bother contacting the retail store because they will inform them. My new position is from eight to four and comes with full benefits, including sick and vacation days and this means next season, I won't miss any of Lucas' soccer practices or his games.

I'm just walking in the door when a ding from my phone alerts me to an email. My heart flutters at Trenton's name asking to set up this nine weeks' parent-teacher conference. Almost all the allotted times he's listed are next week, and since I'm starting my new job, I shoot back an email asking if there are any days this week that will work for him. Almost immediately, he responds asking if today was too short of notice. I reply accepting this afternoon, and ask him to keep Lucas after school since there won't be anyone home to get him. That's the downside of moving here—Clarissa doesn't live across the street to give me a helping hand.

I haven't made this trip since the first conference and this time, I'm all but freaking out. A lot has changed in our lives. I'm trying to keep it together as I pass by open classrooms listening to the hum of the computers.

Trenton is at his desk with a light blue button up with sleeves rolled to his elbows. The moment he glances up, his mouth opens to say something, but he doesn't.

This does something to my chest and to my self-esteem.

He stands with a stack of papers and I scan the room. "Where's Lucas?"

"I sent him to see if Coach Porter needed any help. I told him to be back here by four thirty." He drops his eyes to my heels and then back up. "A retail position has you dressing like that?"

I grin. "Sort of. I had an interview today. I took another position within the company. I start Thursday," I brag.

"Congratulations."

I sit at the table and he begins going over Lucas' grades. Impressively, there isn't a blip during the time where Brian and I split. Trenton said he could tell no difference in Lucas and had no clue until he overheard him and Josh speaking about it. The two class clowns haven't disrupted the class and are quick to help anyone who needs assistance. I smile with pride.

Lucas comes in right at four thirty and stands beside me. "All good stuff, right?"

"Yeah," I answer. "This is your best year yet."

"Mr. B. has a cool way of teaching. He makes it fun."

I smile back to Trenton. "Thank you."

"Did you get the job?" Lucas asks eyeing my outfit.

"I did," I answer proudly.

"That calls for a celebratory dinner. Let me take you both out," Trenton says and I snap my head at him.

"Thanks but—"

"Any place you'd like to go," he interrupts me, smirking with mischief.

"I don't think—"

"Come on, Mom," Lucas whines interjecting my distress.

I rip my gaze from Trenton and look down to my son. "Don't you have homework?"

Trenton stifles a laugh, rocks back on his heels, and crosses his arms looking pretty damn satisfied.

Lucas nods toward him. "Mr. B had me do it before helping Coach Porter. Really makes a difference when the teacher helps you."

Glimpsing back to Trenton, I cock my head to the side and study him. His stare doesn't falter, neither does his shit-eating grin. He's got Lucas on his side and he's using it as checkmate. I'm hesitant. What's his angle? His agenda?

After a long internal battle between my heart and worries, I give in. Trenton offers to swing by the house and pick us up, but I deny the request instantly. I'm not ready to have company, especially *his* company.

We head home to change and get ready for our six-thirty dinner. I trade in my professional wear for something more casual— bluish-gray long sleeve, dark jeans and tall black flat boots. I keep my hair down since it already looks amazing and touch up my makeup. I'm excitedly anxious.

"April, I'm really nervous," I tell her after explaining how I got in this situation.

"About what? You're having dinner with a friend," she says.

"A friend who I know is attracted to me."

"And you're attracted to him. What could possibly go wrong?"

"A lot," I inform her. "I'm not ready to date. Or I don't think I am."

"Who said this will turn into a date? This could legitimately just be a friendly dinner."

"Yeah..." I say in an exhale.

"I think you want this. You're just too chicken shit to admit it. I think you're more ready to date than you think you are."

"No. He'd be a rebound."

"I don't think so. You were over Brian long before you two split. The past little bit has been a readjustment phase. You were used to someone, and now you're alone."

"Are you trying to talk me into dating him?"

"I'm trying to talk you into opening your mind. This may not be anything, but it could turn into something. Don't shut it off and rule it out just because you're afraid."

"I'm not afraid. I just...I don't want to be with anyone," I tell her, trying to convince the both of us.

"Because you're afraid you'll love again. You're afraid of the feeling. I've been there. I know how you're feeling."

"How'd this go from dating to falling in love?" I snort trying to take the edge off the uncomfortableness.

"You're scared shitless of being happy with someone. It's different for you. Scary. You've been miserably strong for years. It's time for you to go have fun."

"Thank you. You know...for being you and being here for me."

"I love you, girl. You've got this. Build your confidence back up and call me if you need me."

Trenton decided on a restaurant that serves everything from chicken tenders to steak and lobsters. He was waiting outside in the parking lot when we arrived and walked in with us. The hostess leads us toward the back and places us in a booth. Trenton immediately takes the seat in front of me but Lucas slides in beside his favorite teacher.

A young and cheery waitress with dark hair pulled into a pony tail approaches the table and gives Lucas a tablet with a ton of games before explaining the specials.

After we order our drinks, Trenton folds his hands on the table and leans up. "This new job, tell me about it."

My chest swells in happiness because someone other than the two main people in my life—Lucas and April—is actually interested, truly interested in a subject of mine. I beam as I delve into my new position, explaining how April had a big hand in it by helping me get my foot in the door and asking all the right questions to help me shine the most. I'm extremely happy about my new hours and how I won't miss any of Lucas' soccer next season.

He listens intently as the green flecks in his hazel eyes twinkle under the soft light. As I express how elated I am to finally have a career that promises me a great future, one that potentially can turn into many other opportunities, the smile on his face makes it to his eyes.

Our food arrives, and even though it slows the conversation, Trenton doesn't allow it to end and continues to ask questions. I'm giddy revealing all the details.

"Oh!" Lucas drops his chicken strip and twists toward Trenton. "I showed coach the way you showed me how to do the triangles. He said next year he might imp...imli...impi..." He shakes his head. "He said he might teach it next year, but he thinks we're too young."

"Implement," he says. "It's one of the best practice drills you can teach. It teaches foot position while keeping your eye out for your opponents. It ranks right up there with dribbling and juggling. I can't believe he didn't teach you guys this."

Lucas shrugs. "Coach says we're just kids."

"Doesn't mean you won't turn into pros. Why not teach you everything?"

"Why don't you teach, Mr. B.," Lucas asks.

"I'd prefer to watch on the sidelines and teach in the classroom," he replies.

Lucas confiscates Trenton's attention with the tablet. Golf and bowling—what man can refuse that? It's funny to watch the two boys overreact and cut up about pins not falling, or the ball splicing...whatever that is. It makes me happy to see Lucas is doing well and not just pretending so I don't worry.

Dinner ends and Trenton walks us to my car. He opens the back door for Lucas but grabs my elbow stopping me from getting in. He tells Lucas goodnight before shutting the door.

His eyes latch onto mine with compassion. "Are you okay?"

"Yes. Thank you for tonight."

"I mean are you okay with everything going on?"

I nod, smiling warmly. "I'm actually really good. Better than I expected."

He scans my face and then scrapes his bottom lip with his teeth before it shifts into the sexiest smile. "Let's go on a date."

I look everywhere except at him. "I, uh, I..." I stutter.

"Just say yes, Riley," he says thickly.

I drop my view to my feet, and he clutches my hand giving it a gentle squeeze. "I'm not out to hurt you. Just say yes."

I chew my lip. "I don't know when I'll have time."

His left brow raises a notch. "Luckily, you just told me your entire schedule. When does Lucas go to his dad's?"

I squint my eyes. "I've agreed to let him go back this weekend."

Victory swarms his expression. "Saturday it is then."

"I—"

"Would love to," he interrupts with a chuckle, putting words into my mouth.

I steady flirty eyes on him and purse my lips. "I would love to," I repeat his sentence.

He grins and squeezes my hand again. "Have a good week. I hope you enjoy it." His words roll off his tongue in such a smooth and sexy tone, my knees feel weak. He winks and takes off to his truck.

I glance to the stars before sliding in my car and cranking it. I thought for sure Lucas would ask why Trenton was holding my hand, but instead he doesn't say a word, which relieves me. I have no idea how I would explain it and I'm not quite sure I'm ready to have this talk.

Chapter 18

My week went by splendidly. After having two days off, and doing absolutely nothing but pampering myself with a lot of couch time, I went into my new position feeling like a new woman. I fell into a perfect routine and for the first time in years, I felt the importance of my job. I was appreciated and needed. I had a purpose, one that didn't involve cleaning the house, cooking dinners, and doing laundry. An inner light of confidence glowed through my first-day jitters and everything came together as if the universe already had it planned for me to have this job. I exuded courage and felt determined. My early mornings and rushed afternoons weren't unfortunate obstacles, but instead they were welcomed perfect opportunities.

I feel proud.

I am happy.

The image in the mirror reflects it and my soul feels it.

I dropped Lucas off at Brian's yesterday after work. I like it better when I do the dropping off because I don't go to the door and it doesn't become a mass of painful uncomfortableness. I'm able to watch Lucas walk in the door and I get to leave without any words spoken between his father and me. It's easier and less strained.

After I got home from dropping him off, I ate a sandwich and did what my body begged me for— sleep...for twelve solid hours.

I woke up feeling refreshed and energized and since, I've been cleaning the house like a mad woman, releasing all my anxious energy on the floor, counters, and bathroom. It's better to expel it in the places needing it the most rather than waste it. My house is sparkling and smells like bleach and glass cleaner mixed with the scent of the vanilla candle burning on the kitchen table.

Excited is an understatement and high-strung is an underestimation. Trenton texted me several hours ago determined to pick me up at the house. Arguing with that man is worse than arguing with a cat. He doesn't listen and will do as he pleases. I finally caved in and gave him directions to get here. This was before I found out he wasn't going to tell me where he was taking me. If I had known that piece of information, I would've used it against him and blackmailed an answer from him.

I finish putting my makeup on and although I don't wear much, I add more to my eyes to give them a bigger pop. I brush out my hair, leaving it down so I don't get a headache, and then slide into my favorite nude heels. I'm dressed casually but sexy, sporting ripped jeans, a rose spaghetti strap tank top with a light gray waterfall cardigan. I'm comfortably classy.

His knock on the door has me shaking from adrenaline and frayed nerves. "I got this," I tell myself, padding down the hall.

Trenton's eyes glow and he grins wide, looking insanely handsome in a turquoise shirt, dark jeans and his chukka boots. He steals my air, robbing it from my lungs.

"You ready?" he asks.

I nod before my words make a path across my lips. "Yeah."

He clutches my hand, leads us down the sidewalk toward his truck, and then helps me in. I'm engulfed by the scent of his cologne—

fresh and spicy—as I watch him stroll across the front of the truck, walking with confidence.

"You look beautiful." He drives off from my house.

I mentally argue with myself. I don't know if I should tell him how gorgeous he looks or if it will tack on extra weirdness already steaming up the windows. I chicken shit out and thank him, fiddling with my purse strap.

The ride isn't long when he pulls into a driveway beside a brick house and then steers his truck past it until the concrete driveway dissipates to gravel crunching under his tires. Lights run alongside the driveway, outlining the way, but where they end, so does the trip.

"Sit there." He jumps out of the truck and strides to my side. "Take off your shoes. You'll break your neck in those heels."

"Why didn't you tell me I needed to change them?" I squeak.

He grins devilishly. "Because if I did, I wouldn't be able to carry you."

I laugh. "You're kidding, right?"

He looks satisfyingly amused. "Come on." He turns giving me his back. "Hop on. Leave your purse and shoes. No one will mess with them."

"Oh my God, you're serious?" I pull off my shoes.

He laughs. "Get on."

I fold my arms around his shoulders before wrapping my legs around his waist. He snakes his hands around my legs and under my knees, pushes the door shut and begins walking along the gravel path. He carries me to the end of the pebbled trail and bends, letting go of my legs and allowing my feet to hit the cool wooden planks that lead the way to a white gazebo overlooking the lake.

The moon shimmers off the water, and lights from houses on the other side reflect in the water as he guides me by the small of my back. Once under the cover of the gazebo, he lights three candles, giving off a picturesque ambiance.

He scratches the side of his neck. "I'm not big on romantic stuff. I didn't plan a big meal or cold wine. I hope you don't mind fruits and beer."

I sit in the corner of the wicker couch and pull my legs into me while he hands me a beer.

"You say you're not romantic, but what is all this?" I take a pull from the cold beer.

He sits on the opposite end of the couch. "I didn't say I wasn't romantic. I'm just not big on it."

"I like this," I tell him panning the view. I look back toward the dark house. "Is this where you live?"

"Yeah. This is home."

"Teacher's pay is better than I thought," I quip and he laughs.

"When I was twenty-one, my dad passed away from lung cancer. About a year later, Mom died. I believe it was from a broken heart. One day she was healthy and the next, she wasn't. She gave up without Dad. This used to be their vacation home and after they passed it was left to me. In the will they specified I had to be twenty-five for it to be released to me."

"I'm sorry to hear about your parents."

A faint smile quirks his lips. "They're in a better place than this crazy world. I miss them, but I still talk to them all the time."

The conversation is too heavy for me, so I jump on the chance to change it. "So, Mr. B., tell me about yourself." I smile tenderly. "What's your story?"

"What's my story?" he repeats.

"Everyone has one and you know most of mine."

He puffs a chuckle and glances at me out of the corner of his eye. "Your story will have a happy ending if I have anything to do with it."

The words startle me.

"What would you like to know about my story?" he asks.

I raise a shoulder. "Tell me about you."

He stretches his legs out in front of him and crosses his ankles. "I'll get the sad and gloomy stuff out of the way." His tone is blithe. "Dated a girl for about four years and just as you've experienced, we grew up and apart. Except she refused to admit it and swore marriage was the answer. I knew better. After some coaxing, we called things off amiably and remained friends afterward. She moved on quickly and got married less than a year later to a man her father introduced her to. She was beautiful and happy that day. Unfortunately, they divorced less than a year later. I helped her move back home with her parents and I haven't talked to her since."

"Wait. You went to her wedding? How did that not destroy you?"

"I was happy for her. Just because we had shared time together didn't mean I was going to bottle up hatred for her. See, we had started off as friends. I used to date her best friend in high school, so we were all pretty close. She cornered me one day and revealed my girlfriend was sleeping with some football jock. Being immature, I broke up with my girlfriend and immediately started dating her. It started off as a revenge relationship. I wanted to rub my anger in my ex-girlfriend's face, but I developed feelings in the meantime. The rest became history."

"Did she know she was part of a vindictive plan?"

"I didn't hide it from her," he says dryly.

"What caused you to fall apart?"

"We grew up. She didn't support my decision to teach. I didn't care for the idea of having kids before twenty-one. I preferred to get my career on the ground instead of trying to juggle a family and college. Fact of the matter, I knew she wasn't the right one for me."

"I like how you're able to talk about it without attacking her."

"Just like you said, everyone has a story. It's how you read it. I could've sulked and basked in the misery of it all, or do as I did and learn a lesson, love, laugh, and grow."

"You're pretty impressive."

He looks to me. "Do you not think you've grown from your experience with Brian?"

"I do."

"And are you sulking or moving on?"

"Moving on, but not everyone would. Some people hold on for dear life."

"You did for a long time."

"I didn't know our time was over before he called things off."

"You tend to see things differently when you're not plastered in hopelessness."

I tip my beer to him. "True."

He grins. "Of course it hurts. Breakups aren't fun. There's always the first initial sting, but once it's gone, so is the pain."

"Even if you're madly in love with them?"

"The pain leaves. The memories are what causes an ache."

"I like your outlook on things," I tell him.

"As do I. Makes things easier if you don't analyze everything and just accept it as it is."

"You've got a special way with things. I especially find it amazing you're able to keep Lucas' attention in class. Normally, he doesn't try and his grades reflect it."

He smirks proudly. "Like he told you, I have fun with everything. Kids enjoy learning through fun, not boring repetitive hard work. And once they prove to themselves they can do it, they become proud of their work, essentially causing them to try harder. I've discussed the changes they'll experience in middle school. The teachers aren't so relaxed. They expect more because the kids are growing, and the kids should expect more from themselves every year."

I'm at a loss for words as I sit and admire him. He's got such a grasp on life and at such a young age.

He turns toward me and drapes his arm across the back of the couch. "Are you good?"

For the first time in a long time, I'm absolutely content with where I am. "Yeah." I grin and take in everything around me. The tranquility of the water. The quietness of the night. The crispness of the air. It's impeccable and much needed.

"Thank you for this," I say.

He traces circles on my shoulder as our eyes grip one another's. Pleasure squeezes my heart and sends flutters along my spine. He leans closer, pulling me toward him.

"There's something between us and I want to know more about it." He rakes his teeth over his lips. "We've both felt it since we first saw each other. I'm not going to play fair," he adds in a low, thick tone, inching his face closer toward mine.

My heart is slamming against my chest, thundering in my ears.

"I'm going to give you my all. I want to make sure I'm the hardest thing you've ever had to walk away from even if it's into the next room. I want to flood your every thought and appear in each of your dreams. Because, Riley, that's what you've done to me since the first time I laid eyes on you."

My air is gone and my mind fumbles for words. I blink back the ardent tears. "I think that's the sweetest thing ever said to me," I breathe out.

His lips tick and he drops his view to my lips but doesn't advance further. He blinks back to me with questioning eyes. I'm on a dizzying rollercoaster and my emotions are hanging on for dear life. I'm terrified, yet my body is buzzing with exhilaration. I feel delicate, like one more gentle stroke from his fingers and my body will splinter into pieces.

"Riley..." His voice captures me. "I mean it." His tone carries a seriousness so deep, I shiver.

He presses his lips to mine, gently and captivatingly. A soft moan escapes my throat as he traces his fingers along the sides of my face, gripping the back of my head. He pulls me deeper into the kiss as our tongues explore, tangling together. A rush of warm adrenaline zips through me. Desire slams my body, crashing against my very existence with the most powerful waves. The kiss is tender, yet incredibly intense. Passionate, yet marvelously violent. And it's the most mesmerizing kiss...

I suck in air when he pulls back and rests his forehead to mine, brushing his thumb over my cheek. I'm weightless from one kiss. His hazels are dark, dilated, and heated. We share the gaze, together trying to gather what we just felt, before he crushes against my lips again. This time it's fierce, like my lips are the last breath he'll ever take.

He glides his hand up my back and splays it across my shoulder blades, digging his fingers into my skin and tightening his other grip in my hair.

A frenzied heat jolts my body, startling the hell out of me and I pull back. "I..." My breathless words fall short of explaining what I feel.

"Fuck, Riley..." His words ride out in an exhale.

I'm lightheaded from the rush of euphoria. He tugs me back to his mouth and feathers a kiss on the side of my lip. "I can lose myself with you." He tugs my bottom lip. "Lose all self-control," he growls, nipping along my jawline.

I struggle for breath. A pleasurable claustrophobia settles and I melt into him.

He grips my cheek, his breath ragged, but something flashes in his eyes and he stops his titillating assault. "I need to take you home."

My face falls. I'm a combination of hurt, confused, and wickedly rejected.

He closes his eyes. "The time will come," he says in a deeply pained tone.

As he carries me back to his truck, he tries lightening the mood by joking around. And even though he manages several good laughs out of me, it doesn't do anything to hush the noisy thoughts. By the time he pulls into my driveway, my mind has taken many turns, dragging me down every dark and negative alleyway, and settles on him not being interested in me.

He walks me back to my door.

"Thank you for tonight," I say stepping into the house.

He tugs me against his body and rests his fingers on my hips, smiling tenderly. "Let yourself feel it, Riley."

"I am," I answer bravely launching a devilish smirk. "The last time you told me that you walked away from me."

"I had to. Being around you was torture. Knowing that you were so unhappy and I could change it for you."

"How are you so sure?"

He bends placing a light kiss against my lips. Suddenly the air cascading my skin feels warmer, but a quiver rushes down my spine causing my breath to hitch. I moan, melting into him.

He pulls away grinning like a bastard. "Because of that feeling."

I'm intoxicated from the kiss, slowly blinking up to him.

"Goodnight, Riley." His voice is husky as he lays a delicate kiss on my forehead.

He walks backward halfway down the sidewalk before he finally releases our intimate and flirty gaze and then turns toward his truck. Inside, everything is frantic—my thoughts, my feeling, my urges. I want to call out to him and beg him not to leave. I want to run after him and throw myself around his neck, but instead, I resist the urges and slink back into the house and shut the door.

Open House

One word—wow.

Chapter 19

Trenton and I have talked every day since our date. Whatever doubts I had after he didn't follow through with what we were feeling have vanished. And although we haven't spoken about it, I strongly believe he did it out of respect.

I don't know where this is going, so I told him I didn't want Lucas knowing yet. It's too new and too early and I don't want Lucas getting attached if things don't work out. He understood and promised to behave and act accordingly.

April went out of town Sunday for a meeting and returned late Tuesday. Then she took off today from work. I've been dying to talk to her, to tell her all about what's going on, so I texted her earlier for an afternoon date.

The moment I walk into the coffee shop, I spot April sitting outside on the bench under a patio umbrella with Josh beside her. She holds up a coffee cup and waves me over.

Whoever built this coffee shop was a genius. They knew moms would need a break from their kids and erected this honey pot beside a park.

"Wish I could tell you this is wine," she quips as I pull out a chair.

Josh brought his soccer ball and immediately springs out of his seat, rushing to the field with Lucas hot on his heels.

"How was your trip?" I ask and then take a sip of the piping hot Latte.

"Oh, the joys of having to sit in a mandatory company meeting," she deadpans. "All part of the job." She sits back and crosses her legs. "Just how long are you going to hold back the details?"

"Of?" I reply.

"You had a date with Trenton and I haven't heard from you since. Either you have been tied up in his bed or tied up in his basement."

I laugh and scrunch my face in excitement. "It was fabulous. Quiet and without elaborate things."

"Where did he take you?" She wipes a drop of coffee from the side of her cup.

"He took me to his house." I say and her eyes widen. "Not like that," I rush out. "He's got a beautiful gazebo behind his house and we shared drinks. He kept it small. It was perfect."

She twirls her hand motioning for me to continue. "And?" The single word draws out.

"We kissed." I try sounding levelheaded but instead I end up in a small girly squeal. "And it was fabulous. But I haven't told Lucas. I want to keep it quiet for a little bit just in case it doesn't work out."

She rolls her eyes. "Don't be so pessimistic. You know this is going to work out."

I cock a brow. "And how would you know?"

"So when's the next date?" She dismisses my question.

"I'm not sure."

She looks over my shoulder and back to me with a smug grin. "So you two are keeping it inconspicuous for a little while?"

"Yeah, until I feel comfortable telling Lucas. I don't want to jump the gun yet."

"You might want to tell him that stalking you will give it away." She nods her head.

I turn and my heart flits. Walking through the front doors of the coffee shop, Trenton strides stoically toward the counter, pulling his sunglasses off his face.

"Ever gotten drunk off a kiss?" I snicker watching him through the window.

"That good, huh?"

I swing my head her way. "Way good. Movie cliché good."

"You're pretty besotted with him. I knew the first day you met him there was something there."

"You didn't know that," I say.

She sits up, leaning toward me. "You forgot your damn name, Riley. I knew."

"So we had an instant attraction."

She shakes her head. "Instant attraction doesn't cause..." She taps two fingers on her forehead. "I believe I said the Earth shifted."

She did.

She stretches her arm up high, waving behind me, and points to the table.

I close my eyes in a bashful fit. "Please tell me you just didn't."

A deep devil may care giggle arise from her chest. "I totally did."

"Hey, Mr. B," April sings in a tone like she knows something she shouldn't. "Take a seat."

I look up to him in all his glory. His eyes shift between us but he doesn't sit. "Hey," he hums and it makes my stomach drop.

"What are you doing here?" I ask with a hushed whisper.

He grins like a bastard again. "Heard the scenery here was stunning."

"Next time, I'm not telling you where I'm going," I quip.

He opens his mouth to retort, but Lucas and Josh run up in exuberance. "Mr. B!" Both boys yell out simultaneously.

"Hey boys," Trenton's tone drenches with delight.

While they talk amongst each other, April gathers her things. She says she needs to make dinner and get Josh ready for school tomorrow, and as much as I love her, I know cooking isn't her specialty. They live off meals made by others—frozen or fresh. Knowing her the way I do, I know this is just a ploy, a deliciously evil plan to have me and Trenton together.

After a few weird goodbyes, she leaves me there with Trenton and Lucas...alone.

"I guess we need to get going too, kiddo," I say.

A dimple appears and Trenton turns to Lucas. "I miss soccer. You up for some play?"

Lucas' little face brightens. "With who? You?"

"Yeah. I can teach you a few things the coach didn't."

I narrow my eyes.

"If it's cool with your mom, I can come over now," he says.

I can't believe he just said that.

Lucas whips his head toward me. "Please, Mom? Please?"

I don't release Trenton from my strangling gaze. "I—"

"I haven't had anyone to play with. Come on, Mom. Please?" Lucas interrupts me, begging.

What else can I possible say to two pleading faces but...

"Okay."

"Can I ride with you, Mr. B? I'll show you where we live!" Lucas blurts.

"You need to ask your mom," Trenton says with a stern, fatherly tone.

Lucas waves his hand at me dismissively. "She's cool. She won't mind."

And that is that. Just before I get into my car, Trenton is hopping in his truck when he winks at me, donning a mischievous grin, and then slides his sunglasses on.

"I'm in trouble," I whisper to myself.

I watch the guys from inside the house as they kick the ball back and forth, occasionally pausing for Trenton to show Lucas a better way of doing things. They both look happy, laughing while they run past each other for their version of a scrimmage.

I continue to sneak peeks as I cut the chicken, toss it in the pan and pour the noodles in the water. Yes, I'm insane to offer an invite for Trenton to stay for dinner, but I want to. I truly like his company and from the looks of it, Lucas does too.

I am in over my head.

I holler out the back door that it's dinner time and they need to wash up. Lucas has never had to be told twice and immediately, he abandons the soccer play, sprinting through the door.

Trenton leisurely brings the ball and hands it to me. He shoves his hands in his pockets and cocks his head to the side running his tongue along his bottom lip. "Figured if we're going to make things work, I need to win Lucas' heart."

I roll my eyes and snicker. "You've had him won over."

"Thanks for letting me come over," he says.

"Where are you going?" I ask.

He throws his thumb over his shoulder. "Dinner time is cue to leave."

"Your plate will get cold then." I smile.

His expression slacks and contentment clouds his view causing my heart to squeeze. I nod inside. "Go wash up."

Other than April, I haven't had company since moving in, and as we sit around my tiny table, I'm highly aware of his presence. We both are unsure what to say or how to act. I'm a nervous fricking wreck, scared Lucas will pick up on the infatuation bouncing between us. I suspect he is too because he's keeping a conversation with Lucas, oddly not about soccer, but about dinner and school.

Once dinner is over, the guys disappear into the living room after I insist they not help me clean. It would be wrong to have company help, besides, he is here for Lucas and not me, right?

I'm washing dishes when Trenton appears behind me. "Lucas went to take a shower."

I smile warmly at him. "He really likes you." I set the last plate in the drainer and turn, drying off my hands and leaning against the counter. "You're sneaky."

He spreads his hands. "What can I say? I needed to see you."

We share a stare—passionate, carnal, and flirty. Vibrations tickle my muscles, hyper aware of the effect he's having on me. I've held my shit together all night and I'm viciously fighting to keep it together now.

He takes a few quick steps and grabs me by the nape, crushing his mouth to mine. He groans when I part my lips, allowing his tongue to slip between them. I slide my hands up his chest as he snakes his up my back and pulls my body against his.

"I fucking crave you," he whispers.

I hum my pleasure while he nips my jawline. Heavily, he drags his hand down my ribs, resting a hard grip on my hip. My mind collides with my body, diving into a lusty heat. And even though I'm frantic to feel him all over my body, my movements are slow. He traces my ear with his lips and goosebumps explode over my skin, sending a quiver down my spine. He releases a deep throaty chuckle before trailing his lips back to mine and savagely giving me a long drugging kiss. As our breaths fall into sync, a vicious urge of sexual desire surges into me. I press against him threading my fingers into his hair.

There's a distinctive creak at the end of the hallway within steps of rounding the corner to the kitchen that gives off a clear and specific warning of entrance. And this very sound has me ripping my mouth from his, lurching out from his arms, snatching a rag, and pretending to wipe down the counter.

Trenton runs his hand through his hair and I nervously study Lucas to see if he caught us. My heart is drumming so hard that my ears are pulsing.

"If you're done with me, I'm going to head out."

I don't know if I'm completely inundated with the fear of being bust, but I swear he added a hidden innuendo within his statement.

"What? Yeah. That's fine. Everything is done." My nerves are all over the place.

Scraping his teeth along his bottom lip, he shifts into the sexiest smile, and before he turns to Lucas, it dissolves. "I enjoyed this afternoon. We'll have to do that again soon. Have a good night." He pats him on the shoulder and starts out.

"If I don't ace the vocabulary test, can I blame you?"

Trenton shakes his head. "You'll do fine."

The door shuts, and I already miss him. Emptiness churns my stomach and I feel like I just lost an important piece of me.

Yeah...I'm in serious trouble.

Chapter 20

Brian picks Lucas up right after school, granting some much needed "me" time. A long bath is definitely mandatory as I take advantage of the quiet house and hot water. When I lived with Brian, I never thought there was a difference between me verses a single mom, figuring I was always alone with no help. But boy was I dead wrong. With Brian surfacing here and there, it offered me a sense of having someone to help on a daily basis, even if he didn't. But now living completely alone, I'm truly on my own and no matter how strong I am, between work and Lucas, I'm tiring out quicker and much easier.

My water stills, ripples evening out and smoothing over as I unwind, picturing my tropical escape. The hammock sways as the warm breeze brushes against my skin. Above me, the fan-like fronds springing from the palm tree rustle gently adding an extra wave-like sound. I am alone, content with the melody of ocean water...

Reluctantly, I get out and make a simple casserole for my rug rat to eat when he gets home. It's in the oven, and I'm wrapped in a blanket, snuggling into the fluffy arm rest of my couch with my e-reader in hand. I'm three words in when the front door pushes open and Lucas strolls in. He places his book bag on the back of the dining room chair and goes straight for the fridge.

"Dinner's in the oven. Don't eat," I tell him.

Brian is standing just outside the door with a perturbed expression. Before I can thank him, he grumbles, "We need to talk."

"All right. What's up?"

He glances behind me. "Somewhere else."

I point to the front porch and start out the door, but he doesn't move causing me to squeeze between him and the wall.

"Lucas told me about his teacher coming over." He leaves it open-ended.

"Okay?" I answer flatly.

"What's he doing over here?" he barks quietly.

I narrow my eyes, crossing my arms over my chest. "Did Lucas not tell you?"

"He said they played soccer and ate dinner."

I nod. "There you have it."

His brows furrow and fire ignites in his yes. "Don't be a smart ass."

Ah...Pissy Brian. "You asked me what he was doing here, but Lucas already told you. Sounds like you're the one being a smart ass. Mr. B wanted to show Lucas a few tricks and play. I didn't see any harm in it. Besides, Lucas already had his mind set on it. I cooked dinner as a way to say thank you."

His eyes settle in a harden glare, and I'm scared to death he can see the truth. "I don't like him coming over here."

"Oh!" I feign giving a damn, placing my hand on my chest. "I'm so sorry you feel that way, but the last time I checked this was *my* house and I get to make the decisions."

"You're on the defense. Is there something going on between you two?"

"What?" I shake my head aggravated he has the audacity to actually give a damn. "No. Brian, there isn't," I lie.

Relief cascades across his face and his nostrils widen as he takes a long deep breath. "I don't want just anyone around Lucas."

"Last checked, I take damn good care of him," I snap. "If you're done, I'd like to go spend some time with my son."

I've got one foot in the door when...

"Do you miss me?" he asks stopping me in my tracks.

I look to the floor and then to him. "I miss what we had, not what we had become."

"You're skirting around my question."

I tighten my lips. "Goodnight, Brian."

I shut the door. I miss when we were younger, not how we've evolved over the years. And nowadays, my mind rests with one man and he isn't being a prick.

"Dad sat in his recliner the whole time," Lucas says with food in his mouth.

Imagine that...

Lucas doesn't say anything else as he scarfs down his food shoveling in fork load after fork load. This is his way of hiding his disappointment and hurt. He doesn't want to talk about it.

The house is quiet. Lucas went to bed about an hour ago, and since, I've been curled under the covers watching TV.

Trenton: I want to see you.

I smile at my text.

Me: I'm free this weekend.

Trenton: Before then.

Me: You make me smile.

Trenton: It's my goal to make you smile.

Me: You're doing a pretty good job at it.

I pray he can hear my how flirty that sounded in my head.

Trenton: I left you something on the front porch.

Trenton: Only go get it when Lucas is asleep.

I eye the text before springing out of the bed and rushing down the hall. I gasp, holding back a yelp when I pull open the door to Trenton standing there.

"What are you doing here?" I mutter.

"Is Lucas asleep?"

"Yes, but—"

He pulls a bouquet of red roses from behind his back. "I needed to see you again."

I'm rendered speechless, blinking back the happiness trying to leak from my eyes.

He grasps my hand, pulls me out onto the front porch, and quietly shuts the door. His lusty eyes latch onto me as he takes my cheeks between his palms and kisses me. I liquefy in his hands being sedated by a feeling I can't quite describe.

He leans back. "I needed that worse."

I stand there lost in a blissful stupor before opening my eyes to his sweet smile. "I...um," I mumble.

He chuckles under his breath and reclaims my mouth. A frenzied heat blasts me and I drop the flowers, pulling him into me.

"Can I come in?" he pants.

"Lucas," I remind him.

"Then come with me to my truck."

I look to the road where his truck is parked and the back to the door.

As if he's reading my mind... "I want to hold you. Lie down with you in my arms and feel you against my body."

No way I can deny that. "Be quiet."

We tread silently past Lucas' room and down the hall to mine. Although I know the boy can sleep through a hurricane, every noise seems to be amplified a thousand times, and it's putting me on edge. I usher him into my room and close the door.

"I feel like I'm a kid sneaking a boy into my room," I giggle.

He smirks with something incredibly lecherous behind it. In an instant, he's against me, running his hands all over my body, missing every spot that's begging for his attention. He lifts me by the ass and twists, placing my back against the wall. A moan slips from me as he pushes his jean-clad erection against me.

He trails his mouth down my neck and slides his hand underneath the hem of my shirt, cupping my left breast. I drop my head against the wall with a soft moan as he kneads my ache.

"Shhh..." he hushes me.

He moves us to the bed, lays me down, and climbs up my body. Pulling up my shirt, he places the most delicate kisses across my stomach and brushes his tongue along my skin. I gasp and arch my back into him when he moves, sucking my nipple into his mouth. He runs his other hand up my arm and grips my hand, holding it beside me.

Pleasure zips through me as he dips his fingers below my waistband and begins massaging my clit.

He pushes a finger into me. "Damn..." he growls, nudging a hard kiss onto my clavicle.

He's ravishing my neck, teasing my nipples, and dragging his fingers in and out of me. I twist, propelling my hips into him as my body begs for more. My core pulses with arousal. A trickle of heat begins at the bottom of my feet and creeps in from every limb. I'm a writhing mess, thrusting hard against his hand.

My orgasm shatters my every sense, jolting a loud vehement burst up my spine. Immediately, he covers my mouth with his, inhaling my moans. Using his whole body, he rocks into me, driving his fingers deeper and me further over the edge.

As I finally slow, I open my eyes to a hypnotic gaze, drenched with fascination and appetite. His breaths are ragged as he removes his fingers and sits up, taking his shoes off. My euphoria slowly dwindles when he tugs the covers down underneath me and lays, pulling me into his body, covering us up.

"Mmm..." he hums. "Go to sleep, Angel."

Do what?

I try twisting toward him, but he squeezes me tighter, stopping me. "Don't worry. I'll let myself out...quietly," he adds.

"Was something not right?"

"Per-fucking-fection," he exhales.

"Are you sure?" I ask, feeling small.

He rolls me to face him and places his forehead to mine. "The first time I make love to you won't be a quiet scene. I'll make sure it's my name that falls from those glamorous lips. Trust me, Angel. When the time is right, you'll beg for me."

How the hell do you respond to that?

He kisses my forehead. "Get some sleep."

I nuzzle against his chest, listening to the beat of his heart as it slowly lulls me spellbound, eliminating my worrisome thoughts. Here, in his arms, surrounded by the scent of his cologne, is a cozy place and I feel safe.

I stretch, feeling unknotted. My bed is a stark contrast from when I fell asleep. Now, it's empty and cold where he had heated it just hours before.

My phone notification light blinks and I reach for it with a giddy grin.

Trenton: The hardest thing was leaving you. Hope you sleep well.

I blush at the text as flash backs slam behind my eyes and my core heats.

Me: I slept splendidly thanks to you. What time did you leave?

Trenton: Not long after you fell asleep. Locked the door behind me.

Me: I really liked my surprise visit.

Trenton: Expect more. I'm far from done with you.

I'm walking on air as I pad down the hallway to start my coffee. I round the corner and am greeted by the flowers he brought me last night, placed in a tall glass with water, centered at my table. My soul contracts with an emotion I haven't felt in a long while.

"Coffee. I need it," Lucas says sleepily, rubbing his eyes.

I laugh. "It'll stunt your growth."

"It'll give me energy," he retorts.

"You're almost eleven. You don't need any more energy than you already have." I grab the orange juice from the fridge and pour it into a coffee mug. "Here. Here's your coffee."

His eyes flick to me.

"Don't you still have an imagination? Pretend it's coffee." I nod toward the cup.

"It's cold," he says blankly.

"Want me to warm it up? It'll taste horrible, but I will."

He stops me from grabbing the cup. "You might make a good villain after all."

I grin, proud of my accomplishment.

"We'll have to work on your horrible laugh." He bounces his finger to me.

I ruffle his hair. "Hurry up so you don't miss the bus." I leave my sweet, sleepy boy at the island as I head for the shower.

Chapter 21

I'm at my desk when I hear the distinctive clicking of heels before the owner of them appears and approaches my desk. "Will you update these employee files?"

I smile up to April. "Sure. Got a minute?"

I'm busting at my seams to tell her about my surprise visit last night.

She frowns. "I wish. Elizabeth has me today...alllllll day today," she drags out. "Is it really important or can it wait for coffee this afternoon?"

"It can wait," I reply.

"If you feel like kidnapping me, I'm good with that too," she snorts and I laugh.

She strolls back out of my office with a natural catwalk, abundant with sway. I've asked her before if she's ever been a model, and although she says no, I wonder if in her previous life she was. I'm not clumsy, but I know if I tried to walk like this, my feet would get tangled together.

The day isn't too long since my work pile extended a bit. I was able to stay focused allowing time to slip away. Before I know it, four o'clock comes and I'm out of the office in a flash, just in time to receive a call from Brian asking if he could get Lucas for a few hours this afternoon. Of course, I won't argue. It's sad it takes us splitting up for him to spend more time with his son.

I wait in the driveway for the bus to drop off Lucas and shuffle him into the car, rushing to get him to Brian's. Thankfully, he doesn't come out when I pull into his driveway.

April informed me earlier she would be a few minutes late "thanks to Elizabeth," so I order her a caramel latte and grab a table. I don't have to wait long before she comes strutting in looking exhausted under her smile.

"Today belongs to the devil," she groans sitting across from me.

"I've heard Elizabeth is a bore."

She rolls her eyes. "A passive aggressive bore. Be glad you don't have to deal with her. So what's the occasion? What brings us to our gossip corner?"

I rub my lips together before speaking, lowering my voice so it doesn't travel to eavesdropping suspects. "Say a man you really like goes out of his way to...um..." I pause hoping she understands, but she looks dumbfounded. I sigh. "What if a guy gets you off but doesn't have sex with you? What do you think that suggests?"

Gah...I feel the embarrassing heat on my cheeks.

Her eyes brighten and she slides to the end of her chair. "Do I know this particular guy?"

I cock a brow. "That's irrelevant."

Commence a knowing grin. "I'd say he's respecting you in a *very* teasing way."

I stare at her without blinking.

"Maybe he feels you're not quite ready to move to the next level?" She shrugs. "What if he's a romantic and wants everything to be right for the first time? Maybe he's waiting to make sure *you're* ready?"

"Why wouldn't I be?"

She takes a sip of her coffee. "Sounds like you had a pretty interesting night."

I bite my lip. "I did."

"Just so we're on the same page, this guy was Trenton, right?"

I puff a laugh and nod.

"He's pretty honest. Did you ask him?"

"Sort of. He said he wanted our first time to be under different circumstances."

"See. I'd say since he knows what you've been through, he's waiting for the right time. Maybe he's scared to move too fast?"

"I don't know." I rub my forehead. "I don't know how to act around him."

"Could be the reason he's keeping things slow."

I drop my hand to the table. "I want to throw myself at him but I'm petrified how Lucas will feel about his mom dating his teacher."

Her brows pinch together. "How did last night happen if Lucas was home?"

I crinkle my nose. "He surprised me with a visit after Lucas was asleep."

"Maybe he thinks he's got an inadequate package?" she jests snickering.

Definitely not what I've felt pressing against me. "You realize he has stopped us twice, right?"

"You're fretting way too much. He's a sweetheart and he knows what he wants. He's probably making sure you feel the same way so it doesn't come crashing to an end before it takes off."

I stare at my cup for a long moment and then giggle. "Are blue balls a girl thing, too?"

"From what you've told me, it's *him* with the blue balls."

"When we were younger, everything was easier and much less complicated. I don't know where he and I stand."

Ugh...I know I'm whining.

"You ask, Riley. Things *have* changed since you were a teenager. However the douchebag won you over, it isn't the same today. Trenton's feeling you out. Throw him a bone occasionally."

"I do."

"Then make that man chew on it." She places her hand on top of mine. "You're difficult to read sometimes, and I'm saying this as your best friend. You need to let him know where you stand, or at least give him some hints. You've been shut inside a void for far too long. Get out of it and tell people how you feel." She stands, throwing her purse over her shoulder. "I've got to get Josh. Do yourself a favor and be in charge of your happiness."

I sit back in the chair and sigh.

I really hate when she makes sense.

Chapter 22

As my week passes, realization of just how precise April's words were haunt me. I've been hiding my head in the sand, petrified to live life, and it's been costing me my confidence and happiness. And the more I think about it, the more I feel like a damn dumbass.

Trenton and I have talked many times over the phone, but I haven't had any more late night surprise visits. I'd be lying if I said I wasn't a bit heartbroken and disappointed. I got spoiled off one night. Hate to see how I'll react to many.

April has planned another cookout, this one much smaller than the blowout she hosted weeks ago. I got here early to help her set up, shared a glass of wine before everyone showed up, and then watched as they streamed in. One in particular caught my eye, and right now he's looking sexy as hell manning the grill. A bead of sweat has formed across his forehead and I watch, sucked into fantasy land as he flips the burgers. There's nothing more arousing than a man cooking.

We share a few peeks—desirable and flirty glances here and there—but nothing too conspicuous since Lucas and Josh haven't left his side. I would feel bad for him, but he seems to be fully enjoying their company while cackling with them.

"Can I spend the night with Josh?" Lucas asks as he throws his plate in the trash.

"You have to ask April," I inform him.

"I did. She said it was fine if it was okay with you."

"Just behave yourself," I say.

"Yes!" Josh exclaims. "Come on. Mom got me the new FIFA game."

And they're gone in a flash.

April strolls up and leans into my shoulder. "He cooks, Riley."

"And looks damn good doing it," I boast.

"Lucky bitch," she titters.

"You've told me before Jeff cooked for you all the time."

"Jeff looked that good when he was younger. This was before age got ahold of him."

This makes me laugh.

She glances behind me and smiles. "Your ears must've been burning."

Trenton steps beside me. "Was I topic of discussion?" His tone carries a faint conceitedness.

"You were," she sings.

He licks his lips and shifts his prideful eyes on me. "So you say? And what exactly were you talking about?"

I don't answer, silently begging April with telepathic thoughts to keep her mouth shut.

Trenton takes notice and rocks back on his heels. "Seems like it was a good talk."

"Sounds like you've recently have had some good nights," April says and I flinch, snapping my head to her in disbelief.

"It was pretty impressive," Trenton says.

I drop my head in my hand. "Oh my God."

He leans closer to my ear and whispers. "I don't recall you moaning that."

I back hand him in the chest.

"You two won't be able to hide this for too long. You're barely able to contain yourselves," April says.

"She has that effect," Trenton tells her, winks at me, and then walks away.

"I don't know what the hell you've been worried about. That man is crazy about you. And he's a damn keeper. It's got to be hard...in more ways than one, for him to respect your decisions, but he's doing it. Do you realize how lucky you are?"

I scrunch my nose. "I'm very lucky."

April makes her way over to a group of her neighbors and I find my way to a few people I've met from her previous parties. I'm not good at socializing, especially with people I don't know very well. There's always the awkward pause and I wonder if I'm interrupting a conversation I'm not supposed to hear. But these women don't skip a beat and continue talking about their kids, but the brunette, the richy one—I think her name is Shelly—switches gears and begins telling them about the new pool boy who just started this week. He's young and easy on the eyes and her husband caught her ogling him the other day. When she states that the other night she fantasized about pool boy while her husband made love to her, I want to puke.

I glance up and suddenly the women's chatter drops into a blurry distance, being overridden by my slamming heart. April's neighbor, Sophia, is talking with Trenton and making it very clear she's interested. She flips her long dirty blonde hair over her shoulder, batting her eyes and smiling her gorgeous big smile at him. She's fricking beautiful—young, perky boobs, beautiful blue eyes, a bubbly personality. And even though I want to knock her teeth down her throat right now, she is really sweet.

She consumes his attention. Every time she laughs, so does he.

Jealous much? Yeah.

"How have you been since you and Brian split?" the red-headed one asks me. I need to learn everyone's name.

"Good," I say.

"Has it caused any difficulties with your son?"

I catch Trenton stealing a peek at me. "No. Actually we get along well co-parenting."

Sophia rubs her hand down Trenton's arm. My stomach churns.

"You should feel blessed. When Jacob and I divorced, we fought worse than we did when we were married."

"We've remained pretty civil," I say.

Trenton says something and Sophia laughs, leaning into him. I stretch my neck from side to side, trying to relieve the green-eyed monster lurking just below the surface.

"It took Jacob and me years to find happy grounds. Does he see Lucas much?"

I know she's only trying to be polite, but she's hitting the highest annoyance level. "He does. We have a good schedule."

Trenton has a beer in one hand, the other in his pocket, when Sophia stretches to her tip toes, placing her face right beside his, and whispers something. Although, he remains emotionless, I can't.

"Excuse me." I muster up a fake smile and rush toward the house.

Lucas is sitting on the edge of Josh's bed, perfectly enthralled with the game as I tell him I'm leaving and for him to behave. He tosses a goodbye over his shoulder without taking his eyes off the screen.

I make my way to April, spotting her not far from where the hellish scene is still playing out, and keep my focus on her.

"I'm leaving," I say. "I can't watch this anymore."

She looks a bit confused before leaning to the side and glancing around me. She rolls her eyes. "I didn't know she would do this. I'm sorry."

I tighten my lips. "It isn't your fault. I need to get out of here. Call me tomorrow when everyone is awake and I'll come get Lucas, okay?"

I'm hurt, sad, and well...angry as hell. Knowing he isn't mine to officially claim, knowing he's fair game to anyone, frightens the shit out of me. And for it to play out in front of me just mutilated my heart. I feel defeated, wronged before I can make things right. I shouldn't care, but I can't deny the feelings I have.

The best thing for me is to try to sleep and wake up with a clearer mind. I squeeze into my pillow, begging the darkness to stop these wicked thoughts when my phone rings.

It's him.

"Answer your door," he says brusquely.

"I'm in bed." Apparently, I'm a little angrier than I thought.

"Get up and answer your door," he demands.

I huff, throwing off the covers and then stomp down the hall.

"What do you want?" I snap, ripping open the door.

His eyes darken. "What's wrong?" But by his tone, he already knows the answer.

"Nothing. I'm just tired," I answer nonchalantly.

His brows raise with amusement and the left side of his lips tick, but he clenches his jaw. "Really?"

I rock back on my heels and before I can say anything, everything happens so fast. He rushes against me, slamming the door shut, and presses me against the wall with his body.

"I hate liars," he breathes, dragging his hand up my arm.

I push it away.

I feel his lips part against my cheek just before he grabs my hands and slams them above my head.

"What's wrong, Angel?" He nips my earlobe.

Sensations. So many sensations.

"Was it the blonde?" he rasps, gripping both my hands under one of his and dragging his other over my shoulder.

My body is hyperaware of his movements. My senses are lost between his touches, the sexual frustration, and the jealous anger.

He hums. "Was it because she was so close, trying to get me to topple into her attraction?" He presses against me, caging me in and grips my hip. "Was it the way she looked at me?"

"I didn't like it," I admit in a heavy sigh.

A deep vibration, a small laugh, thunders from his chest. "Why, Angel?" He grips my thigh and squeezes. My knees fall weak and for a second I'm sliding down the wall, but he stops me. "Because she wants what you want?"

"I..." My mind is humming in a heated charge.

He cups my sex and I gasp, pushing my ache into his hand.

"You what, Angel?"

"You wanted her," I murmur.

He bites my chin and my eyes roll. "You were squirming over it. It bothered you to see someone trying to take what you want." He digs his erection into my hip. "The fucking jealousy in your eyes only confirmed what I've waited so long for."

He captures my lips in a hungry storm, lifting me and forcing my legs to lace around his waist. He starts down the hall, carrying me with one arm as he caresses my breast over the fabric of my shirt. Desperate to feel him, his skin, his touch, I yank off my shirt, quickly ridding me of my bra. He wastes no time lapping between my breasts.

He drops my ass to the bed and, in a swift movement, takes my shorts down my legs. He's out of his shirt and tugging out of his pants with his fervent hazels on me. Suddenly, I feel self-conscience. He's marvelously gorgeous naked with a more profound chest than his clothes give him justice for. The smooth skin of his stomach bears a patch of hair under his navel and travels down. He is all types of divine.

He strokes his dick, biting his bottom lip as I watch fascinatedly. He pushes my shoulder, climbing on top of me, nestles between my legs and begins rocking his dick against my clit.

"Are you on birth control?" he asks impatiently.

"Yes," falls from my lips in a pant.

He lifts, sitting back on his heels, and with his thumb, he starts circling my swollen nub, squeezing my thighs. My hips gyrate on their own accord and I arch, pushing my head into the bed. Grazing his fingers along my skin, he pinches my nipple, and it releases such rapture, I moan loudly.

Continuing the stimulation on my clit, he inserts his fingers and watches me as an enormous frenzied need courses my body, centering deep within my pelvis, and causes my body to contract.

With a grip on my ankle, he quickly shoves his cock into me and I cry out. With my other leg pressed to my chest, he pumps into me and a staggering throb radiates my entire body. Sensing where I am, he slows with long and strong strides allowing me to gather myself, but the arousal is too much.

I dig my nails into his thighs, my hips pushing and pulling with each steady thrust. His breaths are ragged as he shoves into me, picking the pace back up with force, and it begins to draw out my climax. Immediately, he slows again, and he continues this wickedly titillating torture until every smoldering morsel of my orgasm builds.

Unmerciful pulses rip me apart. I mewl, crying out as the earth shatters and explodes around me. Blinding euphoria consumes me. I put a death grip on the sheets and bite back a scream of pleasure.

He slams into me fiercely, burying himself as I lose it under him. Suddenly, his body tenses and he grits his teeth, grunting and rocking madly into me, surrendering to his own orgasm. Inaudible words spill from his mouth, and when we finally reach the end of the glorious ride, he drops to his elbows.

"You're insanity," he breathes.

I'm intoxicated, entirely satisfied, unable to open my eyes. He moves beside me and adjusts a pillow to prop his head up on.

A bite on my ass jerks me from my sleep. Teasing kisses caress my ass cheeks as his hands run along my back. A tickle spreads fire over me when he shifts and grazes his lips up the middle of my back. I moan, trying to turn and face him, but he has other things planned as he pulls my hips, lifting my ass into the air.

From behind, he leisurely sinks his dick into me, filling me fully and then dragging back to the end of his length.

"You're fucking gorgeous, Angel," he groans. "Fucking perfection."

I gyrate my hips, sliding backward into him.

"Fuck yes," he grunts. "Fuck me."

And I do. Shoving backward, I grind into him while he keeps a firm grip on my ass allowing me to please him. I rock against him, my entire body ablaze with a desperate desire.

Abruptly, he rams deep and I cry out from the swell of tantalizing delight. A rumble of laughter echoes behind me and it's both insanely erotic and frightening.

Twisting my hair, he leads my head toward the ceiling and buries himself with a sharp jab. I cry out at the pain, at the intensity, and it unleashes something wild within him. Relentlessly, he plunges into me. He's ravenous.

I buck away at the sting when he slaps my ass and impales with sheer force. Gripping my chin, he leans me up and twists me to his mouth. I'm off balance, resting on my knees as he roots himself upward. Our kiss is sexily sloppy. Our tongues missing one another and our lips hanging on by luck. He wraps a hand around me, holding me hostage as he captures my nipple between his thumb and forefinger and snakes his other hand to my clit, teasing it. It makes my body become insanely greedy and I ride him hard, bouncing on my knees and slamming myself down on him. He works hastily on my nub, drawing out trails of fire from within me. I fold an arm around his neck to steady my trembling body.

We're twisted in an erotic pretzel.

"You're gonna come all over my dick," he rasps. "You're gonna beg me, Angel."

"Yes. Yes," I pant, feeling a bit out of control.

Sounds of our skin slapping together intensify an eroticism I've not ever been subjected to, acting as an aphrodisiac. My moans are rapid and loud. My breaths are quick. He continues to grind into me tweaking my clit.

It starts in my legs, a throb tightening down each muscle, one by one, working its way up until it completely engulfs my body and devours me with a scorching heat.

"Please," I beg, whimpering for more.

He pushes my arm from his neck, forcing me back on my stomach, and grips my hip, surging into me. The sting of his fingers adds a painful pleasure and I bite the pillow.

He succumbs to his orgasm, losing his rhythm, and growls a guttural moan.

I'm trembling, struggling to catch my breath. "Shit..." I can't comprehend a thing. "I..."

Emotionally, I'm done for. I feel exposed, naked from the outside in.

A gravelly chuckle resonates from his chest as he falls behind me and tugs me against his body. "I'm not leaving tonight," he says out of breath.

A tug grips my heart, but it isn't startling. It's refreshing and invigorating as it energizes my soul. I draw his arms around me and squeeze. "I'd like that."

The room has been silent for a pregnant moment when he kisses the back of my head. "You realize you have nothing to worry about."

"Hmmm?"

"My sights have been set on one woman for a while."

My heart dips. "I'm sorry I acted that way tonight."

"You felt threatened. It's a natural reaction," he replies casually.

"Still doesn't give me the right."

He traces his fingers up my arm. "Claim me, Angel. I'm yours."

I can't describe the rush of emotions that just released. It's one that grounds me and lifts me off in flight at the same time. Like riding a roller coaster and having your stomach dip just before cresting the largest hill.

He just rejuvenated my soul with five words...

Chapter 23

"When are we going to tell Lucas?" Trenton asks on the other end of the phone. I haven't seen him since he left the morning after the best night of my life and that was a week ago.

"I don't know," I answer feeling small.

"What are you afraid of?"

"What if you don't like our life? I mean, I have a child who keeps me pretty busy. He's my single most important person. What if he doesn't like it? Or you? And if he does, what about Brian?" I didn't think that completely through.

"What the fuck about Brian?" he snaps harshly.

"Are you okay with having to see him? There's eventually going to be a time you two cross paths," I explain.

"I'm the one in your bed. I'm the one holding you. And I'm the one working for your heart. As long as that doesn't change, I could care less about him. I want in your life, not out of it. We already know Lucas likes me. Now we're down to what if he doesn't like the idea of us dating. And honestly, you'd be foolish to let him decide that."

I pinch the bridge of my nose. "I just don't want to add any more stress on him."

"Lucas isn't stupid, Angel. If you're happy, you know he'll be happy."

"What happens when he gets attached and you leave?" Yet another question without thought.

"Who says I'm leaving? I want to be with you and if I'm not making it clear, I need to step up my game," he says with a chuckle.

"Tomorrow. I'll tell him at dinner tomorrow."

"Am I invited? I'd like to be."

"And what if he flies off the handle?" I ask.

"We'll deal with it when it comes. I'm not sweating that. It's going to be okay. You'll see."

I have felt sick all day today. My stomach has churned, threatening me with throwing my guts up many times today. Efficiency has been out the window since waking up. This morning, I could barely look at Lucas in fear he was able to read my mind through my eyes. I know it's stupid, but this is big—life altering big. And if Lucas isn't happy, it will destroy me. If he isn't okay with me and Trenton dating, it will shred me to pieces and tear my heart apart layer by layer. And although I agree my happiness is my happiness, I want the most important piece of my life to be happy too.

My thoughts are every-freaking-where. I'm making meatloaf with mashed potatoes—Lucas' favorite—just in case. May as well butter him up for this.

I gulp in air when the most anticipated knock on my door sends my heart into a marathon. Lucas glances over the couch at me with a dumbfounded look. We're not used to getting company.

Trenton oozes confidence in his smile when I open the door. Unlike him, I'm in cardiac arrest and sweating like I'm standing beside a fire in ninety-degree heat.

"Nothing to be worried about," Trenton whispers.

"I can't—"

"Mr. B.!" Lucas shouts his elation. "I didn't know we were practicing today. Let me go get my ball." He leaps from the couch, tossing the remote behind him.

"Lucas, wait," I call after him. He skids to a stop and bounces off the wall. I point to the couch with a shaky finger. "Come here for a minute." My voice quivers.

Trenton pats my shoulder as he passes me and takes a seat beside Lucas on the couch. "I'd like to ask you something. It's pretty important."

I'm going to throw up.

"Would it be alright with you if I date your mom?"

Lucas smirks. "Mom always said girls give you cooties. You must really like her." Sarcasm drips from his tone.

I cover my mouth to stifle my laughter.

Trenton chuckles. "I do."

"I'll still get to see Dad, right?" Lucas asks me.

"I'm not taking you away from your dad, ever."

"You'll still be my teacher, right?" he asks Trenton.

He nods. "Won't change a thing at school. I promise."

"Fine by me." He shrugs like he doesn't care.

If there's a stronger word than relief, I just felt it. The world lifts off my shoulders and I don't know if I want to jump for joy or cry, or both.

"Mr. B.?" Lucas looks to his hands. "I don't feel like practicing. I'm tired and I want to be lazy."

Trenton scruffs his hand through Lucas' hair. "Me neither. Hold the couch down while I help your mom with dinner."

He's smirking in triumph when he wraps me in his arms, looking down at me. "I told you."

I rest my forehead on his chest. "It's possible I wouldn't have started dating you if I knew how this day would've felt in the beginning."

He chuckles kissing the top of my head. "Nothing to fret about."

"Please tell me you like meatloaf." My trepidation is muffled by his chest.

"Relax, Angel."

I tiptoe and kiss his cheek. "Thank you."

There's something mystifying about his eyes. They hold knowledge and passion, clutching my heart as I fall into them.

Dinner falls into play, perfectly. It's like life never missed a beat and Trenton has been here the entire time. We share our daily ventures minus my anxious shenanigans, and of course, the boys know more about each other's day since they spend it inside the same four walls together. And when soccer makes an appearance, both become exuberant and gush over it.

Trenton helps me clean the kitchen with flirtatious remarks, dumping the scraps in the trash and wiping off the table. But the moment his hands enter the soapy water and he begins washing the dishes, my knees almost buckle under me—instant turn-on.

"I'm going to leave before Lucas goes to bed," he says.

I give him an ironic glance.

"Several things come into play. First, I want him to see me leave. Second, we both know once we're alone things will quickly become something we can't control."

I'm not enthused by his decision, but I am pleased at him trying to make a good impression with Lucas. That means a lot to me.

He says a quick goodbye to Lucas and places a chaste kiss to my cheek, one that leaves me with an ache because I'm not able to get my fill of him. He winks, and then he's gone.

Chapter 24

Trenton texted me earlier and said he'd pick me up at six thirty, but he wouldn't tell me where the heck he's taking me even when I pressed him with a little ineffective provocative texting. I failed severely. He didn't budge, no matter how much I tried.

I want so badly to tell Lucas not to say anything to Brian about Trenton and me, but I don't feel it's right to teach him to hide things from his dad, so I keep my opinion to myself and drop him off in the driveway without getting out—my normal routine.

Once back home, I rush to take a shower and then change into jeans, a pretty pink blouse, and twist my hair into a ponytail just in time for him to arrive.

His eyes scan over me before settling into a charming grin. "You ready?"

I lean on the door frame, crossing my arms. "Not until you tell me where we're going," I pout playfully hoping to get something out of him.

He turns on his heel and starts off my porch.

"Hey!" I titter. "This isn't fair."

He turns spreading his arms to his side. "Coming or not?"

I snatch my purse from the table and follow him to the truck. "You're not playing fair."

He pulls my hand to his mouth and kisses my knuckles. "Never intended to."

He takes the same scenic route as he did on our first date, down the same windy road, and then turns into his driveway. I don't realize how nervous I am until the moment I step into his house. He clutches my hand and, without a word, leads us through his living room, past his cream colored sectional and out of the French doors to his back porch.

"Trenton..." I trail off.

He's decorated just for tonight, covering a small square table with a gray cloth and centered roses in a tall vase. The sun is on its descent behind the trees, lighting the sky with a deep shade of purple, transforming into a lighter blue, and morphing into a soft orange glow. The lake lies still in the early light of dusk, deepening the romantic ambience and offering a spellbinding backdrop.

From a stainless-steel cooler, just big enough for the bottle, he pulls out wine and pours me a glass.

"It's so beautiful out here," I tell him taking the wine.

"I was hoping you'd like it," he says holding up a finger. "I'll be right back."

He disappears into the house, quickly returning with a tray of fruits and cheeses. "Really hope you're not starving."

I giggle. "I swear you've said before you're not romantic."

"I can be. Take this as a thank you."

I'm bemused. "For what?"

He pulls out his chair and takes a seat before answering me. "Nothing in particular, but everything specifically."

I laugh.

He takes my glass from me, sets it on the table and pulls me into his lap. "For looking at me the way you do and smiling so beautifully."

Yep. I'm blushing.

He runs his nose along my cheek. "I've made it a priority to engross your thoughts. Tell me, Angel, have I achieved it?"

I feather a kiss over his temple. "You have."

"I want to be in your sights even when I'm not around," he says.

A faint smile pulls my lips up. "You are."

"I need you to understand when I love, I love immensely strong."

"Are you telling me—"

He shakes his head. "I'm not saying anything, Angel," he interrupts. "I'm merely warning you for the future."

"What if this is only lust?"

Am I deliberately trying to run him off?

"Do you believe in fate?" he counters.

"I've never put much thought into it."

"The first time I saw you, the floor disappeared. You walked down the hall and rattled my brain for a reason. You fumbled on every nervous word for a reason. Attraction? Absolutely. But attraction doesn't feel like this. Whatever *this* is, it's taken over my existence."

I'm feeling brave as if the guards securing the vicinity around my heart have loaded their muzzles and are determined to protect what hasn't already fallen for him. "What does this feel like to you?"

His eyes dance between mine and his lips twitch. He stands, forcing me to my feet, and hustles into the house with me in tow.

"What are we doing?" I ask following in his wake.

He doesn't answer and continues to guide us through the house and down a long hallway with several black picture frames. I can't make out the images. I try stealing glances into each room we pass, but he's moving too swiftly. I'm not able to catch but a bathroom and a room with workout equipment.

We come to the end of the hall and into a bedroom holding a king-sized bed with black covers tucked tightly and gray pillows lining the top. He spins me in front of him and takes the sides of my head into his palms, crashing into my mouth. His tongue slides along my lips as he backs me up, pulling my shirt over my head. Wasting no time, he undresses us before placing me on the softest fucking bed I've ever felt.

Resting his body against mine, his movements are purposeful and slow, energizing the blood coursing my veins. Soft touches scatter goosebumps over my skin as he feathers just the tips of his fingers along my thighs and up to my palms.

Moonlight peeking through the blinds offers the only light and outlines his figure, concealing his flowing edges into the blackness. The same faint light allows just enough glow for me to see hints of his ardent gaze watching me and seeking something.

He pushes into me, slowly.

Delicate lips and touches ignite a warm, gentle heat to blanket over me. He rocks, pressing his body into mine, his chest rubbing against mine with a blissful friction. He tugs my bottom lip before kissing me slowly and steadily.

There's something behind it—intimacy.

Our breaths are synced with quiet exhales. Our bodies are united, connecting on a deeper level...a soulful bond.

I skim the sharp curves of his shoulder blades as we move together, scraping my fingers down the muscles of his back. Time seems senseless. Each breath holds a purpose.

He clutches my hand and presses it against his chest and for this moment, the beat is so powerful, so robust, I can feel it throughout my body.

He rests his lips against my ear. "What's this feel like to you?" he sighs huskily with smoldering affection.

Profound intimacy, I want to tell him. Falling completely in love...

Instead, I tell him the next thing I feel safe saying. "Cherished."

"Completely," he rasps, continuing to rock earnestly. "And every time I see you, it gets more intense. Further out of control." He grazes my cheek with his lips. "Does this feel like lust to you?"

I rock my head back and forth, unable to voice a damn thing, submersed by the overpowering, conquering passion erupting between us.

One strong heave and I'm overcome with a startling, glorious feeling.

He covers my mouth with his, absorbing my cries of delight and quickens his pace.

My past, present and future sear behind my eyes. Blasts of my hopes, dreams and expectations flash vividly.

"Angel," he groans and it sounds like a silent plea, which slams me back on the ground just in time to witness him lose it, bucking wildly, and rooting deeply.

He drops beside me, breathing savagely, and slides his arm under me, pulling me against him. His heartbeat is fierce as we lie here—my head on his chest, his arm tightly around my shoulder.

He's drawing circles on my shoulder, our breaths slow. "Stay with me," he says into the dark.

I smile. "I was hoping you'd ask that." Truth be told, I don't want to leave. Not after what I just felt. All these emotions are intense, but they don't make me want to run away. Instead, they make me want to run into them without hesitation.

He kisses the top of my head.

"You feel safe," I murmur because I'm still emotionally raw and I want him.

"That's because I am."

I peer up to him, sliding my head on his shoulder. "You always say the right things."

"I feel them. They're not rehearsed, Angel."

"It's different."

"I'm different."

"I know," I say.

"Do you?" His tone carries a seriousness.

"Yeah."

"I want your love, Angel."

My heart stops, or maybe it jumps to my throat, or even drops to my stomach. I freeze without knowing what to say. "You've walked away from me once."

I feel like kicking my ass for saying the first thing that popped in my mind.

"I had to. Even though I didn't want to and it hurt like hell, I did it for you. I know it's hard to end one thing and start another, especially after being devastated, but don't step backward because you're scared. Don't look behind you. I'm not back there. I'm presenting you with a future, but I need you to see me."

"I do," I say softly.

"I've never been afraid to say how I feel, but I protect myself nonetheless. I know the time and place to lay claim to my words."

I don't say anything.

"Let yourself feel, Angel. I see it in your eyes you're scared. Love is scary, but my promise stands. I'm not going anywhere. My plan is to have you. Make *us* something."

"I wouldn't have pegged you to be so sensitive."

"I lost both parents so close together. I learned the hard way to always show how you feel. There are times it's imperative I remain collected. But you'll never worry where I stand with you."

"Where do you stand?"

He rests his forehead to my head. "Beside you."

Silence penetrates our conversation.

I move, placing my head back on his chest and begin trailing the soft skin of his stomach. "He's got the most beautiful hazel eyes with flecks of green that shimmer in the light and are more transparent in the mornings. He has a smile he wears every time I see him and it's the sexiest I've ever seen."

"Who is this?" By his tone, he knows.

I ignore his question and continue while my courage is still present. "I really like him, but truthfully, I'm petrified. I know if it's too good to be true, more than likely it is and I don't know if I'm good enough. I've got scars, recent ones that are still visible. They're mad, ugly, red, and swollen from the fresh lashes across my heart."

"I can promise you the man you're talking about already knows this and is taking his time to dress and nurse the open wounds. He's a patient man who'll wait for them to heal, but as he does, he's going to fall in love. It's out of his control. But I can guarantee you he's holding your hand, tugging you down the fall with him."

I silence.

He squeezes me. "Good night, Angel."

Chapter 25

I wake up alone in an unfamiliar bed, surrounded by his scent embedded in the covers wrapped around me. I stretch and pull myself up taking in the room. The disheveled comforter and our clothes scattered on the floor brag about our mind-blowing night. The blinds are still pulled tightly, but behind them, the night has given away to the dawn as the sun channels through each crack in a vicious attempt to brighten the room.

I gather my clothes and get dressed before setting out to find Trenton. The walls of the hallway hold images of what I'm assuming are his parents. His mother was a stunning woman with soft facial characters, shoulder-length blondish-silver hair and a dazzling smile, but he certainly gets his looks from his father. He's a spitting image minus the salt and pepper hair. Their smiles are the same. The mischief in their eyes are identical.

As I continue down, the pictures begin to tell the life of his family. Trenton was an only child and his parents adored him. They took many trips, most of them by the water. When I end the hallway, Trenton is leaning against the sandy-color granite counter holding a cup of coffee. He appears small in the large room with dark cherry cabinets and stainless steel appliances.

He grabs the coffee pot and pours the dark liquid into a green mug before handing it too me. "Good morning."

I smile. "Good morning."

"Did you sleep well?"

"I did. Did your mother love to cook?"

His brows pinch together, pulling close with bewilderment.

I gesture my hand around the kitchen.

He shakes his head. "Dad did. His favorite spot in any house was the kitchen and he adored cooking for Mom." He rolls his eyes to the ceiling. "I didn't get the cooking gene. I can grill, boil water, and pray everything tastes good, but making a meal portraying what a world-class chef would falls numb on my fingers."

I giggle. "No wonder it's been finger foods."

He pushes off the counter and kisses my cheek. "I can always take you to a five-star restaurant."

"I'll take pinwheels over the price of those restaurants any day."

He laughs. "Unfortunately, I wasn't expecting company, so unless you want a breakfast bar, I have nothing for you."

"I'm usually never hungry in the mornings."

"What time do you have to get Lucas?" he asks.

"Brian usually brings him home before supper time."

He nods. "Anything in particular you'd like to do today?"

"Spend time with you for a little bit," I say feeling bashful yet brave.

Ah, the smile that caused. "Lazy Sunday it is. Come on. Let me show you around the house."

I was right last night. There is a room dedicated to workout equipment. He recounts how it used to be his dad's office where he'd escape to write his sports column while his mom sat and did crosswords. It was her favorite pastime when she wasn't spending time with Trenton. He said she always told him crosswords were what made and kept her mind sharp.

There's a guest bedroom, which holds more items from his parents—his dad's favorite writing pen, a portrait his father had painted of his mother...

"They adored each other," I think out loud.

"They were madly in love. Had been since fifth grade. They lived a block away from each other and Mom always bragged how Dad would get up early and walk her to school. I grew up watching them live out their fairytale as Mom called it."

I smile at the thought. "My parents were polar opposites of yours. They only loved each other and in a very private way."

"You don't talk about your parents much," he states leading us back to the living room.

"I don't have much to say. They turned their backs on me and haven't contacted me in almost eleven years. They've never met their only grandchild."

He doesn't say anything. Coming from parents who adored one another and him, I'm sure just the thought alone perplexes him. It took me a long time to accept that my parents wanted nothing to do with me. But with bad experiences come lessons and values ingrained. I will never turn my back on Lucas regardless of the troubles he'll face.

Trenton dropped me off about an hour ago, leaving me with a soft kiss and a slow goodbye. I didn't want him to leave and by the way he was acting, he didn't either. But unfortunately reality comes back and makes its presence known.

I shower and then start a simple dinner—spaghetti—my go-to, easy meal. Ten minutes before five, Lucas comes bursting through the door and throws his bag on the couch.

"Hey," I call out, tossing the rag on the counter.

"Hi." By his tone, there's something wrong.

And before I can ask, in walks Pissy Brian, uninvited and with angry eyes. "He's mad because I wouldn't buy him a three-hundred-dollar paintball gun because it 'looked cool.'" He air quotes.

I swing my head to Lucas. "Since when did you start liking paintball?"

He shoves his arms across his chest. "Since seeing it on TV."

I raise my brow.

"Doesn't mean I'm buying you an expensive toy," Brain objects.

"It's not a toy," Lucas protests in a yelly-voice.

"When you start showing more interest, we'll talk about it. Until, drop it. It's not going to happen," Brian says sternly and then redirects his glare to me. "I need to talk to you."

Those words are starting to lose their seriousness. They're beginning to be a conversation starter rather than a dreaded thing to hear.

I tell Lucas to unpack and cool off with a quick shower and then join Brian on the front porch with his pissy eyes and crossed arms. Typical Brian.

"Lucas tells me you're seeing his teacher," he spouts.

Dammit. I'm going to have this conversation much sooner than I prefer. "I have."

"Are you fucking him?"

I flinch drawing my brows together. "I don't see where it's your concern."

"I knew there was something between you two. You were fucking him while we were still together."

I glower at him. "I was completely faithful to you."

"I don't want him around my son. And if I have to I'll tell the school—"

I throw my hands to the side. "And tell them what? That you're jealous?"

"Keep him away from my son," he barks.

"And if I don't?"

His eyes snap flashing a malicious anger. "You will."

"Just because you're a raging asshole doesn't mean you can control me anymore. I'll do as I please when I please and *how* I please. I'll never intentionally hurt my son."

He gives me a once over, puffing out his chest. "You've gotten ballsy."

I stand up taller, holding my ground without words.

"I'm still his father."

I nod. "You are and I'll never take that away. You're a good dad." I want to spew hateful words. I want to so fucking badly...

"I'm serious, Ri. No other men around my son."

"I'm not going to live my life alone. I don't expect you to either. Didn't think your little plan all the way through, did you?" I belittle him.

"Are you fucking him?" he grits.

"This conversation is over." I start back in the house when he grabs my arm causing pain to shoot to my fingers.

"I'm not done talking," he seethes.

I jerk my arm out of his hand. "I am. Goodbye."

I shove through the door and slam it behind me, scared he'll follow.

I rub the sting from my arm. "Asshole," I breathe out. I don't move until I hear his SUV crank and scream away from my driveway.

I push off the door, make our plates, and sit at the table waiting for Lucas, trying to calm down and not stew over his attitude.

Chapter 26

The week went by quickly and without any more instances from Brian. When he dropped Lucas off on Wednesday, he didn't come to the door like he normally does. I was grateful for it too. After he confronted me, I stewed on it for days without meaning to. I ended up telling Trenton that Brian threatened to run to the school. He laughed it off and said it was a last-ditched empty threat and he wasn't worried about it. Just to add a layer of peace of mind for me, he spoke with his principal. The principal said as long as it didn't interfere with teaching, there wasn't a sign of favoritism, and he kept things professional, he couldn't do a thing about it. There isn't a rule established concerning us.

Trenton came up with the idea of making tonight a movie night with Lucas. I love the idea except we can't agree on what movie to watch.

Lucas springs to the door after hearing Trenton's signature light tap and snatches the door open. "Tell Mom we are *not* watching her movie. Tell her to watch Batman Vs. Superman."

Trenton steps in the house toting a bag. "What movie does she want to watch?"

"Some cartoon," he grumbles rolling his eyes.

I greet Trenton with a kiss on the cheek. "We've watched Batman too many times to count. Finding Dory will be cute."

"You're an adult, Mom," Lucas says as if I didn't already know.

"And animated movies are great for the whole family no matter what age," I say.

"They're for kids, Mom," he declares candidly.

This causes Trenton to chuckle. "How about something different?" He pulls a box out of the bag.

"Twister?" Lucas asks bemused.

"It'll be fun. Help me move some stuff." He pats Lucas on the shoulder and starts sliding furniture out of the way. I figured Lucas would protest that as well, but instead, he jumps right in and helps.

I can't tell where bodies start. We're a tangled mess with our hands and feet on various colors. My butt is in the air. Lucas is a twisted frog. Trenton is a pretzel with half his body across Lucas' and one leg between mine.

Steadily, he reaches out and flicks the spinner. "Right hand green!"

"How the heck am I supposed to get past you?" I ask Lucas. "You're hogging the whole thing!"

Lucas giggles and turns his head trying to look up at me hoovering over him. "I'm going to win. This is all strategy."

Trenton takes advantage of Lucas and I bantering and slides his hand past mine taking the only green spot closest to me.

"This isn't fair!" I crack up, stretching my hand between Lucas to the next closest green.

Trenton flicks the spinner again and bursts in laughter. "Left leg blue.

Lucas does it with no problem since he's young and stretchable. It helps he isn't in a compromising position too. Trenton quickly nabs one but is sweet enough to leave me the closest one. Just as I start,

Lucas adjusts below me, pushing his back into my chest and knocking me off balance. I topple down on top of him.

"You took me out!" Lucas cackles.

"You were trying to sabotage me, so you better believe it." I'm in stitches cracking up.

I pop popcorn while the boys put everything back and then take a seat beside Trenton on the couch. Trenton settles the debate about the movie and adds the two interests together—*How to Train Your Dragon 2*. Lucas has seen parts of it but has never watched it all the way through. I fell in love with the first one so you can imagine my excitement to know there was a second one.

"Mr. B.?" Lucas hasn't adopted Trenton's name. He says he feels weird calling him anything other than what he's used to. "You're coming to my birthday party, right?"

"Of course," he answers.

"Making sure," he says nonchalantly.

Trenton squeezes my knee, smiling proudly, and I rest my head on his shoulder.

My little family is starting to pull together and I love it.

"Love you, kiddo. Have a good weekend."

Lucas climbs out of the car tossing his bag over his shoulder. It's Brian's weekend. "Love you."

Brian jogs toward the car, holding up a finger. He stops and says something to Lucas and then strides to my window and bends. "Do you mind if I bring Lucas home late Sunday?"

"How late?"

"Around eight? You won't have to worry about fixing dinner for him. I'm gonna take him to a restaurant in town so he can meet my girlfriend."

You'd think that stings. It didn't. Not even a sliver of jealousy pangs my chest. No waves of envy.

"Don't do it out of spite, Brian. If you're certain things are serious, that's fine. But if it's just a random hook up, please don't drag our son into a malice war against me."

"There isn't a war between us." His tone is casual, but his eyes hold an evilness. "Since you introduced him to your boyfriend, I figured it was a good time he could meet my girlfriend."

"As long as you're certain she isn't just a fling—"

His eyes flash wide with anger. "You introduced him to yours." His tone is childish. "What's the big fucking difference?"

"Trenton went to our son and asked for his permission to date me. I didn't spring it on him. Besides, they're not strangers."

Anger shifts into rage. Something flares in his eyes, something I didn't see coming—hurt. "I'll do it my way. I don't need my son calling the shots."

I smile warmly because if I don't, I'm going to get pissed and I know my next words will hurt him deeper. "You're right. I don't either. But we raised our son to protect his momma. He's doing a fine job. Please don't have him around a bunch of different women. It won't teach him any respect."

He slams the palms of his hands on my door. "Does this not hurt you?"

"Is this what this is? Who can hurt who? I'm not playing that game with you, Brian."

"Ri, I don't—"

"Just do the right thing for Lucas and *not* your selfish ways," I cut in with a softer tone. "Text me and let me know when to expect him." I reverse out of the driveway, finished with this rotating conversation. It isn't leading anywhere.

He scratches the back of his neck, his expression defeated as he watches me drive off. I'm not going to listen to whatever it is he has to tell me. I made my decision long ago. I'm done.

Instead of making plans with Trenton, I planned a much needed girls' night with April earlier in the week. Josh is with his dad and I'm curled up in her sofa chair with a glass of wine while she sits on the couch. It's quiet. No kids. No men. Just us.

"Brian is introducing Lucas to his girlfriend Sunday," I tell her, pulling the attention away from the television.

She blows a breath. "He finds out about Trenton and now all of a sudden he has a girlfriend."

I cock a brow agreeing.

"Do you believe he's got one?"

I shrug. "Don't know. Don't really care."

"Would it bother you if he did?"

I shake my head. "No."

She takes a small sip of her white wine. "You know witnessing it is much different than being told about it."

"As long as he doesn't hump her leg in front of me, I don't think I'll be bothered by it."

"Are you ready to see it? Him with another woman?"

"It's not like I didn't know the day would come. I hope she makes him happy. He needs that. I hate we wasted years of our lives trying to be that person for each other, but seriously, I'm happy for him."

"Uh-huh?"

I stifle a laugh at her unconvinced expression. "I'm serious."

"That's good. It's a good sign. Are you going to be okay when his girlfriend has to pick up Lucas?"

"Provided the bitch won't try to steal my mom status, I'll be just fine."

"And how does Trenton feel about all of this?"

Just mentioning his name spreads heat full of adoration to comfort my soul. A faint smile tugs at my lips. "He does well keeping a straight head."

"You're pretty smitten over him," she says.

"Uh-huh," I hum before swallowing my wine.

"Enough to admit you're in love with him?"

This makes me beam from ear to ear. "To you. Yes. Madly. To him? Not yet."

"What the hell are you waiting for?"

I raise a shoulder. "Right timing? I don't know. Sometimes I feel it's perfect. Other times I worry he's not there."

"Your head must be stuck up a baboon's ass. He's crazy about you. I think you're scared."

"Chicken shit," I admit. "I haven't told another man I lo—"

"Annnd right back to Brian," she huffs, dropping her head to the back of the couch.

"Have you? Have you told anyone you loved them since Jeff?"

She levels her view. "I haven't had a serious relationship. My Mr. Perfect hasn't shown up."

I shake my head in a condescending way. "You have no room to talk then."

She drops the conversation—she has to. She knows I'm right. She turns her focus back on the television. I feel triumphant. I finally silenced Miss Always Right.

Chapter 27

Mother Nature has blessed us with a gorgeous day. It isn't hot, rainy, windy, or cold. The weather is perfect for Lucas' birthday party. We've had it at the soccer complex for years and I'm not about to change it this year just because of small mishaps.

Lucas is on the field, kicking the ball, playing a small game of soccer with several of his friends. Most of them are soccer players as well. Another group is shooting basketball and a select few are playing on the playground. Shouts, squeals, and playful banter rush me from all angles and it relieves me to know everyone is having fun. Like my separating from Brian was going to impact their lives.

I know—ridiculous.

Trenton is also out on the field with Lucas while April helps me set out all the plates, silverware, and snacks. She sets Lucas' cake shaped like...you guessed it, a soccer ball, in the middle of the table.

"Brian not coming?" April asks.

"He will," I say hopeful. He's going to crush Lucas if he doesn't. Surely he's not going to miss his own son's birthday.

Out of the corner of my eye, I see April stiffen and suck in air. "Uh, Riley? Did you know he was going to bring his girlfriend?"

I wrench my head behind me. Lucas told me about her Sunday night after he got home. *She was pretty, but not as pretty as me,* although I know it was a bias opinion. *She was weird like she was uncomfortable. She looked really young and had an annoying laugh.*

One thing's for sure—she's definitely beautiful and way over dressed. Her black hair is long and flowing, curling toward the ends of the strands. It shines and I can bet she has the hair most girls envy, not experiencing bad hair days. Hell, I think I tame the dragon locks when I shove my hair in a bird's nest on top of my head where she probably wakes up with top-notch everything.

"I'm pretty fashionable, but who wears dresses like that to a kid's party?" April whispers behind me.

Her teal sundress chokes her tits, forcing them to sit pretty and perky while sinking her waist line in and releasing off her hips.

"Maybe she's afraid someone will steal her man," I deadpan reverting my attention back to the chores at hand.

"You okay with this?"

Honestly? I want to puke, but I smile. "I'm good," I try convincing myself.

She narrows her stare, holding me hostage as she quietly picks me apart. I can tell she wants to call my bluff, but she doesn't and I'm so fucking thankful she leaves it alone.

I hear Lucas yell something out and I look up just as Trenton strolls past Brian and his friend without paying them any attention. Brian glowers, his expression hardening along with the grip on her waist watching him come toward me.

Trenton grins and kisses my cheek. "You okay?" he asks breathless.

"I am," I lie.

I am not. Most definitely am not. Adrenaline from an indescribable weirdness has me hiding my shakes.

He glances up to April as she leans closer. "Just so you know, you have evil eyes on you. Either he's stabbing you to death or burying you alive. Whichever he chooses, he isn't happy about you being here," she whisper-snorts.

"He needs to turn his attention to his son instead of worrying about me," he replies. "What can I do to help?"

"Can you grab the ice out of my car? It's in the orange cooler," April tells him. When he rushes off to get it, she elbows my ribs. "Get your shit together, Riley."

I'm trying to be collected, but I'm afraid everyone can see I'm losing myself. Being in the same vicinity, both of us with new partners, not together, feels really...really...really fucking awkward. I stand with Trenton on one side and April not too far away on the other side, watching Lucas finish the friendly scrimmage game so we can start passing out the cake.

Brian's pissed eyes are latched on to me, his jaw tight, lips thin as he scowls behind the head of his friend. Hell, she's too preoccupied with her nails to give a damn anyway. Behind my own sunglasses, I pretend not to see him, disregarding the hairs on the back of my neck standing up.

Trenton squeezes my clammy hand and bends to my ear. "Are you sure you're okay?"

I smile up to him. "It's really weird," I finally admit.

The right side of his lips pull up, but he doesn't respond.

Brian keeps his distance as Trenton and April help me pass the plates of cake out to the kids. I feel like he's standing back, waiting, before he pounces. And I'm right.

I'm shaking like a leaf when he strolls up wearing the fakest smile possible, leaving his girlfriend at the end of the covered area. I extend two plates with cake and ice cream on them.

"Didn't I tell you I didn't want him around Lucas?" he grits still sporting the bogus smile.

I jump slightly, but plant my feet. "Don't." I warn in a hushed tone. "Not here."

"Fuck that. I told you I didn't fucking want him around and you're going to blatantly disrespect my wishes," he spits quietly.

It catches Trenton's attention and he steps beside me tucking me into his side "Not here, man. Not in front of the kids. Celebrate today with Lucas," Trenton says calmly.

I'm shaking so badly that my knees don't feel like they'll keep me up much longer.

Brian sizes him up. A fire bursts behind his eyes. "This doesn't have anything to do with you."

"Why don't you make *it* about Lucas and handle your personal business elsewhere." I swear if I wasn't already in love with him, this would be my pivotal turning point.

Brian scrapes his teeth along his lips and is about to say something when Lucas comes bouncing up. My heart is thundering in my ears. I'm scared Brian will show his ass in front of him.

"Dad? After that," he nods to the plates, "do you want to kick the ball with me?"

I don't know if Lucas saw what was happening before coming over and is trying to put out the fire, or if this was an innocent question. Either way, I want to kiss his face off.

Brian's expression lightens. "We'll see, bud." He glances back to Trenton with a malice intent. "Maybe *Mr. B.* would like to get out there with us?"

I want to bury my head in my hands.

Trenton smiles. "Thanks, but I can play with Lucas anytime. Besides, he's already beat me twice today."

I rub my chin and bite my cheek trying to hide my laughter.

"You've taught him well," Trenton adds and then takes a drink from his red solo cup and tops it off with the most smartassed smirk.

"Lucas, Dad will play after they eat some cake." I break the intense conversation taking place directly before my son. "Finish yours. I'm sure by that time, Dad will be ready."

I sigh in relief, letting go of a breath I had no clue I was holding when he skips back to the table, unaware of what's going on.

Brian walks away also, having been beaten at his own game with class.

"Is it just me or is the air out here really thick?" April chimes in trying to lighten the mood.

It isn't helping. I'm nearly shaking out of my damn skin. Before I can gather myself, Brian strolls right the hell back up with his arm around his girlfriend's waist and the largest malicious, shit-eating grin. "This is Alex."

Her name causes a dip in my stomach and I lean into Trenton to keep my balance. Hurt splinters my chest.

She giggles a nervous high-pitched noise. "Actually, my name is Alexandra. Brian's the only one who calls me Alex."

"Hi." My voice cracks and Trenton begins to circles a finger on my lower back.

"I'm Riley, Lucas' mom."

She looks at me like I'm nothing important, like I'm trash sitting by the door waiting to be thrown out.

Brian eats my reaction. His jaw is ticking with a vindictive, spiteful pride as I flick my horrid view between him and her. His brows twitch with amusement. My throat tightens.

I twist my lips. "I'm glad you could come," I tell her praying for strength.

April bebops around me and sticks her hand out. "I'm April. Her best friend. So, are you from the escort service he was telling me about? I thought he was crazy at first, but man, look at you." She steps back examining her. "Do they have men as good looking as you?"

Prayers answered.

The disgusted horror in her eyes is superlative.

"April!" I hiss quietly trying to hide my laughter.

She looks to me innocently triumphant and shrugs. "I just wanted to know."

When Alex scampers off with hurt feelings, I pinch the bridge of my nose. "I cannot believe you just did that."

"She was stinking up the joint. Both of them were. Now, he'll do damage control for a little bit and leave you alone with his vengeful ways."

I drop my hand. "And what if he comes back *re*-vengeful." I emphasis the beginning.

"I think he'd be a fool," she says.

Trenton remains quiet, a stoic, emotionless expression resting on his face. This scares me. "Are you okay?" I ask softly, rubbing his bicep.

There's something in his eyes, something I can't put my finger on, but he blinks it away. "I'm fine. Are you? You're shaken up a bit."

I strive for a genuine smile to hide my true nerves. "I'm good. Thank you for stepping in."

He places a chaste kiss to my forehead and squeezes my shoulders. "I wasn't going to let you deal with that alone."

I'm surprised to see Brian leaving. It's as if he's admitting defeat, running from the very fight he started. But it also allows my world to settle back down. For the rest of the party, I don't have to watch my back and worry he'll pounce. From the haughty expression and the evilness in his voice, I know exactly the "Alex" he introduced me to and why. But *she* isn't the *he* he'd made her out to be.

After everyone trickles out, Lucas and I head back to the house with Trenton not far behind us. He's been tight-lipped since the Brian incident. His demeanor, although relaxed, appears to be tense like he is fighting within himself to remain collected. It's the closest I've seen to him losing his temper.

He comes through the door carrying a bag and toting a grin. "Chocolate cookies and cream for the birthday boy since he hasn't had enough sweets." His lips spew sarcasm and he places the tub on the counter. "And I have a sneaking suspicion, mint chocolate chip for the woman blindsided today and in need of a pick-me-up to hold her off until I get my greedy hands on her body tonight."

I thread my arms around him. "You're hailed as a hero in a woman's world."

He winks. "Ice cream. The go-to soother for every woman. Where's Lucas?" He scans the room.

"Shower. I told him he smelled like a construction worker who's forgotten how to apply deodorant." I laugh.

He rests his hands on my shoulders. "You looked a bit rattled. Was it the girl? Or the way he acted?"

"Both. But the girl threw me off. He used to get calls in the middle of the night from someone named Alex."

"You think he cheated on you?" he asks.

I walk away and drop into the corner of the couch. "I don't know."

He takes a long breath and then joins me, staying at the opposite end of the couch. "I don't know what to tell you."

"It would make sense. You know? The changes. The attitude."

"Would it make it easier for you to understand?" he asks.

I tilt my head. "I don't think it matters at this point."

"I'd say it's in the past and you should be moving on into the future. But from my stand point, you're snagged now. There's many unanswered questions swirling in that beautiful head of yours."

"I just...I don't know. Maybe I need to talk to him?"

I glance up to him. Hurt has made a very clear presence in his eyes. Worry is seeding deeply behind it.

"What will it help if you do?" he asks.

Before I can answer, Lucas comes into the room.

"I got ice cream," Trenton announces, patting my leg and getting up to get it.

My phone chirps and Trenton hands it to me with an agonizing glare.

Brian: I really need to talk to you. Call me.

I glance back up to a darkened set of eyes. "Will it upset you if I call him?"

I witness a possessive anger flash in his eyes. He tightens his lips. "No." His single word is engulfed in hesitation.

I close my bedroom door, leaving Trenton and Lucas in the living room, and sit on the side of the bed. Taking a deep and unsteady breath, I slide my thumb to his name.

"Hey," Brian answers with tenderness. "Listen, I'm sorry."

"You put me in an awkward situation," I tell him.

"Seeing you with him..."

"Was she the Alex who used to call you at night?"

There's a pause. "Yes. But there wasn't anything going on."

"You lied to me for a long time. You led me to believe she was a man," I say.

He huffs out a breath. "When Lucas told me you had a new boyfriend, it pissed me off to know you could move on. I didn't think it would, but it did. I stooped to a new low and wanted to get back at you. I wanted you to feel the gut wrench I felt, so I called her."

"Way to adult, Brian."

"I never claimed I was perfect, Ri."

The line falls silent. I'm chewing my lip staring at the corner of my dresser.

"Ri?"

"What?" I answer.

"I miss you."

The words catch my breath. Moisture begins gathering in the corner of my eyes. "You've been such an asshole."

"I don't know how to handle this," he says despairingly. "I thought I was doing the right thing when I called it quits. We were so miserable. You were. We didn't get along. Instead of putting extra work into us, I pussied out and took the easy way."

"I tried," I remind him.

"It hurts to hear about you with someone else. Someone who makes you happy. I lie awake at night wishing it was me instead of him. I messed up, Ri." The line falls quiet again. "I fucking hate knowing someone else...I just fucking hate it," he growls under his breath.

"You wanted this," I say.

"I don't. Not anymore. I want you. I want us."

"Then why were you with Alex and when did this start?"

He exhales and I can picture him pinching the bridge of his nose. "It was new. A change. New attention. Flirty things. I got wrapped up in it."

"I need to go." I'm desperate to not hear anymore.

"Is he there?"

"Yes."

"Ri, I'm sorry. Today was a low blow and instead of hurting you, the pain I witnessed in your eyes rocked my heart and brought me to my knees."

"Guess you got a taste of what you did to me, huh?"

"If I could rewind everything, I would. This...it's not me and you know it. I'd rather flower you with love than throw shit in your face. Somewhere I lost myself. It took me feeling this pain and jealousy to get it. I don't want this anymore. I want you. Here with me. I want us back."

The sense of desperation dripping from his tone overwhelms me. I close my eyes. "I loved you with everything I had. It wasn't good enough for you. I've never experienced a hurt like the one you handed me. It devoured me. You made me walk away from someone I loved, from something I worked so hard for. And in the time we've been apart, I realize just how empty I truly was."

"Can we have dinner one night? Talk some things through."

I don't answer.

"I still love you, Ri."

"I've got to go, Brian." My voice quivers.

"We weren't a thing, Ri. I called everything off on the way home."

"I'm sorry to hear that. I'll talk to you later."

I don't wait for him to say anything else and hit the red "End Call" button. Then I drop my head into my hands.

Holy shit...I feel numb.

Trenton and Lucas are on the couch laughing when I pause at the end of the hall watching them. Trenton notices me first. His smile falters, and his eyes begin to question me.

I'm scattered. I don't recognize my own thoughts.

"Grab a spoon and join in," Lucas calls out.

"I'll start dinner in just a little bit. I don't want to spoil it," I lie. I'm not hungry. My appetite disappeared when Brian started delving into his emotions.

"About that," Trenton holds up a finger. "I'm cooking."

I arch a brow. "You are?"

"My specialty. Pizza in a box."

"Mom does that sometimes, too. Says it's from a special restaurant." He leans in close to Trenton and whispers. "It's from the pizza place."

Pizza was delivered and the boys devoured it. I managed one slice, but I couldn't stomach any more. Lucas went to bed an hour ago, leaving Trenton and me to ourselves in the living room watching a movie. I haven't paid any attention to it. My mind is long gone, drowning in a tidal wave of its own thoughts, mostly of Brian and Alex. It's all I can think about.

"Talk to me, Angel." He squeezes my hand. "What was said when you called him."

"He apologized for being a jerk," I tell him without emotion. My body feels lost in a void.

"That was nice of him." Regardless, if he tried hiding the flippancy in his tone, he failed.

"It was the same Alex."

"You need to remember where you were heading. I'm doing my best to be patient, but this," he waves his hand over my body. "You being lost somewhere else is testing me. I detest knowing I'm sitting beside you but not the one on your mind."

I dig my palm into my forehead. "I'm sorry. It was just a lot to take in."

"What? Today or the phone conversation?"

I can hear him restraining anger.

"All of it," I admit.

"It's dug up some emotions in you. What did he have to say?"

I rake my hands over my face. "He misses me."

He swallows hard. "How do you feel about that?"

I stare out in front of me and faintly shake my head. "I don't know."

He pops his knuckles, inhaling a deep breath. "I'm not going to sit here and work hard for your heart, patiently letting your wounds heal, just for you to go back to thinking about him. I'd love to take you to your room and remind you exactly where you belong, but I'd be a fool. It would be a waste of time. Your mind isn't with me, and I shouldn't have to remind you."

"No," I exhale. "I'm okay."

"Angel, that was a weak attempt to convince yourself. I hate knowing how great our future looks, but it's getting fucked up by him. And there isn't a damn thing I can do about it."

He stands and pulls me into his chest, wrapping his arms around my waist. "My words will only be confirmation to what you feel, but I don't need them to fall on deaf ears. It's up to you to either hold on or let go."

"I don't want to let go." My voice breaks as my throat begins to burn, holding back the tears.

"But?"

I try to back away, but he tightens his arms around me, locking his eyes on mine. "Riley, this isn't a conversation I'll let you just walk away from." He lowers his voice into a deeper tone. "Don't let him confuse you with words."

Tears slip from my eyes.

He shakes his head. "I don't use words. I show you everything. Where I stand. Where I want to be. I never leave a doubt in your mind. I don't ever want you to second guess me. Did you feel that with him? Did you feel cherished and safe?" he bites. "I'm promising you a happy ending and I damn well intend to give it to you. You deserve to walk around with the smile you've been wearing. I can't help you do that if he's crossing your mind instead of me."

"I...I don't know what to think about all this." I begin to cry.

"What's there to think about?"

"He..." I stop, glancing toward the ceiling, urging my tears to slow.

"Words, Angel. All he's ever given you are words. Pay attention to actions. Mine are fucking clear. Don't look behind you. Don't look where you've been. I'm standing in front of you *again* begging you to see me."

"I do see you," I say.

"What do you see?"

"Happiness," I tell him.

The corners of his lips twitch but then he frowns. "Then why the hell am I standing here begging you to be with me?"

"You aren't."

"Then tell me, Riley, what the hell am I doing?"

I blink away my tears bringing him back in focus. "I think I need a break."

His hazels flash wide with anger. "He devastated you and he's about to do it again."

I shake my head. "I just need time to think."

"About what?" he snaps. "What exactly do you need to fucking think about?"

I blink.

He exhales a frustrated breath. "You don't need a break. You don't need to think. You have the answers. You're just not listening. He saw how you looked at me. How we are as a couple. That's his driving point behind all this. Jealousy is eating him alive. He's willing to tell you anything you want to hear. He doesn't want you to move on without him, but he expects to move on without you."

"That's not fair. I—"

"I warned you I don't play fair, Angel."

"I didn't say I'm going back to him. I just..."

"He's succeeded with words. To clutter up your thoughts and wipe me out of them."

I look down to my feet when he finally releases me.

"I filled the empty void that he left with happiness, hope, and intimacy. *I* gave you a new reason to smile. You gave me a fucking reason to smile. I give you all this for that fucker to waltz back in and steal it away. Those tears...you haven't done that since I've been with you. They're the last things I ever want to see on your face. And if he was man enough to admit it, he'd know you are in better hands than his. Instead, he wants to make sure everyone around him suffers. It's a fucking shame your next devastation will be delivered by your own hands." He fumes.

He starts toward the door and I call out. "Don't leave."

A sad smile contorts his lips. "I don't have much to stay for."

"I never said I didn't want to be with you," I sputter through tears rushing toward him.

"If I did my job right, you wouldn't need time alone. I'd be the very person you run to." He places the softest kiss to my cheek and then disappears behind the door.

I gulp between my sobs. The vison of the door morphs into a black blob through my tears. Desolation crumbles around me and I fall to the couch, dropping my face into my hands, and bawl.

Why is this happening to me?

Chapter 28

Today—morning sucked. Work sucks. Last night sucked. Yesterday went by as a scorching blur. I was a zombie, a vacant lifeless shell walking around the house while being forced to give Lucas an imitation smile. And when night fell, I feared sleep. As I laid with my pillow tightly against my chest, my heart ached, personal sorrow rained around me. I cried harder than I ever have, unsure the direction I should go.

I came to work without a smidgen of focus. I feel like broken glass with sharp edges, shattered and without reason. Tired of fighting it and needing a friend, I head to April's office. She looks up from her papers when I knock.

"You got a minute?" My voice trembles.

"Shut the door behind you. What's wrong?"

"We broke up." I begin to cry.

"What?" she exclaims jumping from her seat and rushing to me. "What the hell happened?"

I tell her what happened from the moment Trenton and I got home to Brian's phone call and where it ended with him walking away. My hands are clenched tightly in my lap, tear drops splashing them.

"You've gotten yourself into one fucked up situation. What does your heart say, Riley?"

I glare up at her from underneath my wet, matted lashes. "If it was that easy, do you think I'd be here..." I spread my arms. "Here in your office crying?"

"Want to know my opinion?"

I nod, dropping my head back down.

"Set up a meeting with Brian. Not at the house. Somewhere in public. And you two talk about everything that needs to be talked about. Get every damn thing out in the open. Once it's there, you'll know what to do."

"You think so?"

"But you have to hold on to reality, the realness of it all. Don't fall into deception. Don't seek something that's nonexistent. You need the raw truth to burn you."

Friday

Today's the day I told Brian I wanted to meet him.

I've wandered through this week suffering from an agonizing torment threatening to devour my existence. Dodging questions from Lucas about Trenton all week has been difficult. Having to pretend all is okay and that we're just busy has added additional distress.

I drop Lucas off with April and she lights a fire in me with a small pep talk—*Don't fall for smooth words and unjust actions. Demand answers and feel your heart out. Most importantly, look at him. Really look at him.*

And it's the very thing I plan to do. I want answers. I deserve them. My heart requires them.

I'm a basket case as I stroll into the little burger joint ten minutes away from April's. Brian smiles somberly when he spots me and hugs me as I approach the table.

"I'm glad you called me. I got you a tea," he says.

Now that I'm here, I'm not so sure I completely understand why.

"You look good."

I sharpen my eyes. "Don't try to butter me up. I didn't come here for that."

He folds his hands on the edge of the table. "I'm not buttering you up. It was a compliment from my heart."

"I want everything to be truthful. I've earned it."

"I promise." He nods.

"What happened with her? Was she the reason everything changed?"

His brows raise. "We're jumping right into everything?"

I cock my head to the side glaring at him.

He gets the warning. Utter understanding and complete vanquish saturate his expression. "She's the secretary for the steel company. We cross paths a lot and on a normal basis, we speak daily." He pauses, running his thumb through the condensation on his glass. "The thought of being with someone else, what it would be like, and would it be any different started consuming me. We had been together for so many years, everything had become stagnant. It left me wondering if there was something else."

And to think I laid in bed with him.

"Did anything happen between you two?"

He glances away, diverting his attention to anything but me. I don't budge. I'm not going to.

He stretches his neck. "Not at first. I don't know what happened but one day I kissed her."

That stings.

"I regretted it. Damn I regretted it. But as the day went on..." He bounces his head from side to side. "I took her out to lunch that day and made out."

That fucking stings.

"After that, I knew what I did was wrong. I never wanted to put myself back in the position because you meant more to me than to screw it up like that. I didn't tell you, but God knows how badly I wanted to. I wanted to confess everything. You deserved to know, but I was petrified of the outcome."

"How long did I look like the idiot?"

"It's not like that, Ri."

"Explain to me what it's like."

"I missed our excitement. I tried finding it with you, but our schedules never balanced out."

"I was a stay-at-home mom. A fucking housewife, Brian. My schedule was always the same," I quietly grit out.

"I hated watching you try so hard to fix us and despised myself for causing so much disruption."

"You used to lie in the bed and promise me the world. You swore you wouldn't ever be that guy who cheated. But here you are confessing."

"It's not like I slept with her."

There's always subtle indications. Being with him for so long, I learned all of him, his body movements, the slightest change of habit...I might have been blind as fuck when I was with him, but I'm sitting across from him with a clear head, and I see exactly what I need to see.

"What stopped you from sleeping with her that day? I know it wasn't me. I was the farthest from being on your mind. So, what stopped you?" I squint, belting him with an intrusive stare.

"That doesn't matter."

I lick my lips and lean in closer. "What. Stopped. You?" I ground out each word, one by one through teeth clenched so tightly, it sets my jaw ablaze.

He drops his view. "Dad walked up to the truck," he answers melancholy.

"Your dad?" I question disdainfully. "Not me, but your dad. Not your son or your family at home, but your dad?"

"Shit just happened. It got out of control. I don't have a good excuse."

"I'd say. You've been with her since we split," I say straightforward.

Smugness spreads on his lips. "What's happened since we've split is none of your business."

My jaw ticks with an anger. I'm not jealous. I'm mad. Mad that I'm just now finding out the very person I slaved my heart and soul to disposed of it like it was nothing. I meant nothing in a time of temptation. I'm so unimportant, my respect I've earned was hurled aside.

"What about you?" he asks.

"Me?" I snap, pointing to myself. "Well, I was at home keeping it together so you could go gallivanting around with your dick."

He closes his eyes in frustration. "How'd you and Trenton come about?"

"I had the decency *not* to cheat on you." I smirk like the devil. "Besides, what's happened since you kicked me out isn't any of your business."

If looks could kill, I'd be hanging in a meat locker.

He rubs his chin. "I've made my mistakes. I've come clean. I want you back. I want us back, Ri."

I twirl my straw in the tea between the chucks of ice watching a tiny tornado rush through the liquid. Even with him in front of me, only one person rests on my mind—Trenton. My heart is beating for him and I'm here wasting my time with Brian.

I pull my purse into my lap. "I let way too many years pass by as I stayed devoted to you. You stopped respecting me. You quit loving me when I never did. I worked. I tried with all my might to keep us together, but it was all in vain. I wasted so much of my damn time off in an imaginary illusion. I love where I'm at now. I wake up every morning knowing I'm no longer exhausting myself with a man who only says he loves me. That matters to me. Because of you, I threw away years I could've given to someone that I mattered to." I bite off bitterly, standing and tugging the strap of my purse over my shoulder.

"I want to marry you," he jerks to his feet.

I smile as tenderly as I can possibly muster. "I'm glad you never asked me. All this time apart was the best blessing I could've ever asked for."

He snatches my arm turning me back toward him. Intense eyes dart between mine. "Do you love him?"

It's a sobering question. I pull my shoulders back, ripping my arm out of his hand, and set my jaw. "Yes," I answer truthfully.

Me: Call me please.

Me: I need to talk to you.

I've tried calling and texting Trenton but all of them are going unanswered. I had a revelation while I listened to Brian explain how he threw everything away over boredom. I realized, I'd never do that to Trenton, and I know without a doubt, he wouldn't let things run stagnate between us. He would never let me doubt where his heart lies. So much that he hasn't even told me he loves and I already feel it in my every heartbeat.

I'm frantic as I drive to his house, disregarding speed limits and zigzagging through traffic. Cars are smears, houses are ink blobs.

I yank my car into his driveway and slam my Honda in park, racing toward his house. My feet pound the sidewalk and then bound up the steps of his front porch.

I'm out of breath when he finally answers. "I don't need to think," I say. "I know my answer. It's been in front of me. It's you. And I want to be with you. I know this more than anything."

The muscles of his jaw tighten before he speaks. "What makes you so sure?"

"I met with Brian today to talk. And all I could think about was you and how I was wasting my time hearing what he had to say instead of spending it with you, someone who means something to me. Everything that came out of his mouth meant nothing. *You* make me feel. *You* give me a reason to smile. It's been you putting one on my face and allowing me to carry it even when you're not around. It's been you the whole time." I'm desperate for him to understand the sheer sincerity.

Emotionless, he hasn't moved.

"I don't want anyone else. I want you. I know that now more than I ever have. It's so clear."

His lips form a straight line. "I'm sorry, Riley. I can't compete with a past you continue to look back at. I—"

"I'm done looking back," I plea. "There's nothing back there. You're in front of me. I want to be with you."

He clears his throat and peers at his feet for a fleeting moment. When he looks back up, my world begins collapsing around me as I see the pain about to be delivered to me. "I don't, Riley. Things just won't work out between us. I'm sorry."

"What?" I choke.

The door shuts causing the black paint to conquer my only view of hope. My chest constricts, extracting the air from my lungs. Numbness clouds my body, spreading to my feet like a wildfire. Broken torment shatters my heart, leaving it in pieces.

I gasp, but no matter the amount I try taking in, I can't catch my breath. A painful confusion slams into me like a searing bolt of lightning, projecting a reckless weakness and spiraling out of control. I stumble backward and somehow make it to my car.

I don't know how I got here, behind the wheel. I don't remember starting my car or backing out of his driveway. Hot streams singe my cheeks. I shouldn't be driving.

"Sooo, how'd it go?" April answers singing.

"I—" I choke trying to form words through a strangled throat.

"Riley? What's wrong? Are you okay?" I can hear her panic, but it's muffled. "Honey?" she calls out for me again.

"Trenton's done with me," I sob. "He doesn't want to be with me."

"Where are you?" she rushes out. "Pull over. I'm coming to get you."

"I just left his house," I weep.

"You don't need to drive like this. Pull over. I'm on my way to get you."

"Can Lucas stay with you?" I manage to say.

"Yes. Of course. Are you sure you don't want me to come? What happened?"

The light turns red and I stop, dropping my head to my steering wheel. "I want to be alone," I say as my breath begins leveling out.

"What happened?" she repeats.

"Trenton said he didn't want to be with me," I snub, my voice forlorn. "I'll get Lucas tomorrow."

"Call me if you need me. You sure you don't want me to come over? I'll call Jeff and—"

"I just want to be alone. Please."

Chapter 29

The past two weeks have gone by like a fog settling on the San Francisco Bay. I can see the lights, but they're out of focus with silhouettes in the distance. Brian has left me alone. No calls. No texts. Nothing. And I couldn't be more grateful for it. I only talk to him when he picks up Lucas. He carries a different tone, one proving he's come to the conclusion of the damage done and there isn't any hope. I'm assuming Lucas told him about Trenton and me breaking up. In an odd twist, he apologized saying he screwed up my happiness again. I would've believed his remorseful apology if his eyes didn't carry happiness. I wanted to smack him, but I took the high road and accepted it.

It wasn't his fault. It was mine. I should've realized what I was doing before actually doing it.

I haven't contacted Trenton regardless of the ache to. Even on the nights I'm wide awake, staring at the ceiling, or crying into my pillow, I resist the urge. The heartbreak is devastating and now I completely understand what he meant when he said it would be me delivering it to myself. I hate myself for it. I hate my thoughts got muddy. My hurt has been unbearable.

In the dictionary, the word emptiness is defined as the state of containing nothing; vacant or unoccupied; hollow and meaningless. Nowhere does it state the severe abundance of pain, reverting into an erosion of one's deprived heart.

One last look in the mirror and the reflection lies. I resemble a young woman in her late-twenties, happy and ready to have fun. My hair is in a high ponytail and I'm of course, dressed comfortably casual with a brown long-sleeved shirt and tan heels. But if you look closely, underneath the makeup covering the worn-out appearance and dark circles under my eyes, through my fake smile, you'd see the truth. I'm completely broken.

April honks and I gather my things, heading out to her. A sexy but soft perfume immediately surrounds me when I drop into her Mercedes.

"You're looking good," she says.

"I'd say the same about you but I can't see you through all the perfume," I snort, trying to make myself get in a better mood. This wasn't my plan to go out, but she strong-armed me into it, leaving me without a choice. Besides, that's what friends are for, right?

"Smells fantastic, doesn't it. We had it on sale so I ordered a bottle."

"Is this the two-hundred-dollar bottle you were grumbling about being too expensive?"

She cuts her eyes at me playfully. "It. Was. On. Sale."

I laugh. "No judgement. Splurge away! It smells good."

"Exactly why I bought it," she says. "There's a quiet bar downtown. It isn't too loud. We can dance if we want, or hang out at the tables in the back. I thought it would be perfect."

"Do they serve liquor?" I deadpan.

"They do."

"Then I'm down." If she's going to force me out, I'd like to
hunt for my smile at the bottom of many glasses. It has to be there
somewhere.

And of course, she's right. This isn't your typical night club.
They have music playing and a dance floor, but it's separate from the
tables off in the back. And although you can still hear the music, it isn't
so loud you have to yell over it. My body isn't being slammed by the
deep hits of bass, or ears bleeding from the loud lyrics. And I'm
relieved to see college kids aren't running amok.

The bartender...gah... That man either has eyes of a God or
contacts. It's criminal to have bright blue eyes of that nature. And his
tousled inky black hair only complements them more.

We found a table closer to the front, but far enough where we
still don't have to yell over the music. April sits where she can keep an
eye on the dance floor. "Just because you're not here to get picked up,
I'm ready to be swooped away."

"Mind if I join you, ladies."

He's got long brown hair, disheveled mixed with spikey, a
beaming white smile sitting on a jaw that hasn't been shaved and a white
shirt unbuttoned at the top under a blazer jacket. You'd think if he's out
to nab a hookup, he would've put more effort into his looks.

I can't get past the patch of hair clawing out of the top of his
shirt.

"Sure!" April chimes and scoots over.

I'm glad. I wasn't moving.

"How are you ladies tonight?" he asks with a failed swoony
voice, darting his eyes between her and me.

"Great," April says before his gaze shifts to me waiting for a reply.

It takes all I have not to roll my eyes. I take a sip of my rum and coke and allow it to burn a smile across my lips. "Peachy."

"It's the first time I've seen you ladies here," he says.

I don't like him. Nope. Not one bit. "So you come here often..." I swirl my hand insinuating for a name.

"Oh. I'm sorry." He laughs nervously and I've deemed him a douche. "I'm John."

"So you come here often, *John*?" My voice is flat.

April bugs her eyes at me when he isn't looking and this causes me to give in to my eye roll.

"Not too often."

"Then it would make sense why it's the first time you've seen us here then, huh?" I grumble.

He looks to April, back to me, and tilts his head. "I hope you have a better night," he says and leaves.

"Will do!" I call out behind him.

"What the fuck was that?" April hisses.

"I didn't like him."

"You need to lighten up. Just because you're not here for anyone doesn't mean I'm not. Calm the inner bitch," she says. "How'd you not like him when he didn't get one sentence out before you sank claws in his neck."

"The curly pubes popping out of his collar." I start off strong but end in a giggle fit.

"Oh my god, that's disgusting," April chortles.

"It has the exact same texture as pubes. Twirl it in your fingers. No difference," I jest.

"I'll never look at chest hair the same."

My laughter dies down as a familiar sensation begins crawling at the base of my neck. Heat tumbles over my skin contradicting the annoying chill shooting down my spine. Quickly, I scan the crowd, checking from the bar to deep into the dancing bodies, but I come up empty handed. I rub the back of my neck trying to relieve the sensation, but it isn't going away.

"He's gorgeous," April sighs, and I turn following her stare.

April and I have always had different taste in men. Her being six years older, she prefers an older man in his mid to late thirties and well dressed, one who doesn't mind suits and ties. In order for them to win her heart, they must look good clean shaven with an incredibly nice smile. I, on the other hand, prefer a more casual look, less upkeep so to speak. I don't care if they shave or not, but if they have a beard, it's got to be well-groomed and not wild outback woods hunter style. I don't care to nuzzle against a hibernating bear.

But, for once, the universe has lined it up for me to agree with what she's looking at. He has to live part time in a gym with the way his red t-shirt is hugging his body, showing off his oversized muscles. From this distance, he looks like he could be a surfer, with messy dirty blond hair and a damn good looking smile.

"He just turned twenty-one," I quip twisting back to her.

"Old enough to let me show him a good time," she purrs. "Just because I'm in my thirties doesn't mean I can't have fun. Thirties is the new twenties."

"Then that makes him a teenager," I snort.

"Quit being a Debby Downer. If I want to dream. Let me chase them."

I snicker. "Go ahead. I'll refill your drink and have it ready for you to cry in when he calls you Mom."

She drops her head back and laughs loudly, flirtatiously too loudly, and I can only assume she's trying to catch his attention. I dig my palm into my forehead.

"You have the maturity clubbing level of an early twenties woman," I tease.

She wags her brows. "I have the sex drive of one too. He can call me Mom in the bedroom as I spank him for being naughty." She claws the air chewing at her straw.

"Why?" I whine my laughter playfully. "The mental image. I can't erase it."

She gives me a big, toothy grin. "He won't call me Mom. I'll be back."

She strides off, leaving me alone with the wicked picture of her with a whip and him over her knee. I shake it off in time to experience another pesky feeling of someone watching me, but I don't acknowledge it. I mean, the place is crawling with people.

Dragging my finger across the rim of my glass, another voice says hello, startling me.

His smile catches me first—crooked, up to no good, but smooth. His eyes are naturally squinty, or at least I think so. Either that or he's over playing the "Hey, I'm really freaking cool" look with his black leather jacket.

"Hi." I grin, sitting back.

"I'm Michael." Without invitation, he sits across from me and places his beer on the table, stretching his hand out for me to shake.

"Riley." His grip is firm and wet. Completely sweaty as hell. I don't let my smile falter in disgust as I tuck my hand under the table to wipe the moisture off on my pants.

"You're way too pretty to be sitting here alone."

I scan over him, trying to find something about him I don't like, something I can bitch about, something I can focus on to give me reason to dislike him, but I can't. There isn't anything. No pubes poking out from under his shirt. No acne. Nothing. His cheek bones are defined and even his lips are cute with the bottom thicker than the top.

I throw my thumb over my shoulder. "I'm with a friend. She just took off on a prowling hunt."

"Want to dance?"

I shake my head pulling my drink to my lips.

His eyes squint even more. "Bad night?"

"That obvious?" I ask even though I know the answer.

"You don't seem happy to be here."

I scrunch my nose. "My friend dragged me here."

"You too?" I watch relief relax his shoulders. "My boys told me about this place. They hyped it up all week long."

"She didn't tell me until I got in the car."

Oh, the unruly smile I just unleashed from him. "My friend doesn't have a car. I was forced to drive mine. I didn't know what to wear."

I know this scene from *Deadpool*...

"At least you have something to wear. I had nothing. These are all her clothes." I point to myself.

"My mom bought me this outfit."

"At least you have a mom. My mother disowned me when she found out her little angel got pregnant."

He chuckles. "Do you watch a lot of movies?"

I purse my lips. "Straight out of *Deadpool.* Do you always use it as a way to pick up girls?"

Satisfaction settles his expression. "No, but I've always wanted to do it. You just took my virginity."

I almost spit my drink out. "Glad to be of assistance. I think."

"So, you have a kid?"

I nod. "Yes. He's eleven."

His head flinches back. "You don't look that old."

"I was eighteen when I had him."

"Explains it. And did your mom really disown you?"

I run my tongue over my teeth. "Yep. Couldn't believe her child was having sex after years and years of preaching how it was the devil's tango. I was an embarrassment, so out the door I went."

"Is the father still in the picture?"

I read between the lines. "In my son's, yes. But not in mine."

"I—"

"Leave you for one minute and I'm replaced," April interrupts, toting the gorgeous guy in the red shirt beside her. She points to him. "This is Nick."

Michael smirks up to him. "I'm Michael and I know this loser." He looks back to me and tips his head at his friend. "This is Nick."

I grin up to Nick. "Oh, the friend with no car."

Nick's eyes shift between us. "It's in the shop."

April scoots in beside me as Nick sits beside his friend. Come to find out, they're brothers, with Michael being the youngest at a ripe old age of twenty-four and Nick toppling the charts at twenty-nine. Neither look a day over twenty-one. Life has treated their skin as a precious gem. They're fun to talk with, personalities are laid-back and entertaining.

"Would you ladies like to get out of here and grab something to eat?" Nick asks after about an hour.

I kick April under the table in a vain attempt to telepathically say no. But instead, "Sure," she chirps.

Well, that worked like a charm. I smile at Michael and pull a shoulder up. "Where at?"

"Choice is yours. Greasy food, deli, or the Italian restaurant around the corner," he says.

"I prefer the deli," I answer.

"Greasy food is for hangovers. Italian restaurant is a date. Let's do the deli," April agrees.

I convince April to let the guys drive themselves and us follow them. My imagination can always get the best of me if I allow it to, and tonight, I've allowed it. As we drive there, I explain my reasoning—just in case. What if they turn out to be serial killers and we're stuck in their car? What if they break down and need a ride home? What if they kidnap us?

April laughs at me, but I'm serious—people are fucking nuts nowadays.

This place has the best sandwiches. I used to come here for their Tuesday specials but haven't since I moved out and got my own place. Fresh breads, freshly cut meats, the crispest veggies...it's delicious.

"What do you do for a living, Nick?" April bats her swoony eyes.

"I'm a physical therapist and a personal trainer," he answers.

I almost jump out of my seat at my victory of pegging him as a gym rat, but I remain unexpressive.

"Michael?" she asks.

She catches him with a mouth full of drink and he rushes to swallow. "Machine operator. Nothing fancy," he says dismissively.

I'm trying to pay attention to the conversation, really I am, but my mind is as far away as possible thinking of nothing in particular. Okay, I might be fantasizing about being snuggled in a warm blanket on the couch watching *Deadpool* thanks to our little banter earlier. It's been a long while since I've seen it.

Michael's nice, but I'm not interested. This isn't doing anything to spark the want to care either. But April is interested. She's feeding into their every word like they're serving her sugar on a golden spoon, sprinkled with sexual neediness. She's the cliché of every tasteless romance movie—flipping her hair, batting her eyes, touching arms, and listening intently. They're eye-candy. There's no denying that, but regardless of how many times she's told me I need a good fucking to get everything off my mind, I'm not interested in the loveless flings.

I'm not ready to be back on the playing field. I want to drown in my depression. Sink in my self-loathing for just a bit longer. It might

be dark and lonely down here, but there is some positivity seeded in it—
me. I'm learning about me. Finding myself. Everything Riley. She's
always done for everyone else, forgetting herself in the process. The last
time I knew myself, I was eighteen with a newborn baby in my arms. In
those days, I devoted my life to my son and my boyfriend, and that's the
last time Riley was spotted. I've been missing ever since.

"You okay?" Michael places his hand on top of mine snapping
me out my thoughts.

I quit pushing around the grains of salt scattered on the table
and pull my hand out from under his and into my lap.

As I glance up to him, I almost yelp but instead it comes as a
squeaky gasp. My heart stops and my stomach sinks. A hot flash bursts
in my gut and spreads outward toward my fingertips. A lump forms in
my tight throat.

Hazel eyes are steady on me. With an arm stretched, Trenton
watches with an unreadable blank expression as he uses two fingers to
turn his cup in place.

My luck...

I swallow my heartbeat and move my view back to Michael.
"Yeah. I'm fine."

I drift back to Trenton, soaking everything about him in a quick
peek, before ripping my attention back away from him. I'm glued
staring at the water ring my glass has produced in front of me. I'm not
looking back. I'm scared to. Petrified of what I might see. I'm still
emotionally unstable, and hot stings are threatening my eyes.

I grab my phone from my purse.

**Me: Please don't make a big scene, but I'm going to get out of
here and grab a cab.**

April: And leave these hotties?

Me: They're sweet but I'm not interested.

April: Have you seen their muscles?

Me: You can tell me all about how they look naked later. You'll thank me for leaving.

She stifles a giggle. I knew she would.

April: Do you want me to take you home?

Me: I'll call a cab. You do feel safe, right?

April: They're harmless. I was hoping a night out would knock you out of your funk.

Me: Look to your left.

Her mouth falls open and she whips her head back to me. "I didn't know," she says out loud.

Both guys, ignorant of our texts, glance from her to me. I fake a smile and spew the first thing that pops in my head. "I just reminded her I need to get my son really early in the morning," I lie. "I need to get going."

"I'll take you home." Michael begins to pull something from his pocket.

"No!" I rush out. "I'm good."

Confusion dawns in his expression. "Can I call you sometime?"

"I-um." I sigh. I'm done pretending. "I'm not ready to do the whole dating thing. Long story. But I had a great time tonight. Thank you for adding to it." I glance to April as I stand. "Love you. Text me when you get home."

My main goal is to get away from the restaurant as fast as possible without running. Running requires effort and in these heels, screw that. Plus, with my luck tonight, I'm likely to break an ankle.

The night carries a quietness in the air even when noises envelope around it. The streets aren't busy contrasting what the daylight hours present. Normally, the sidewalks are packed with individuals entering and leaving the shops littering the city blocks. The air is crisp, feathering cold kisses across my bare skin...winter is coming.

The road carries cars past me. The street lights illuminate the pavement beneath them with an eerie, evil burn of red before quickly blanketing them with a refreshing and calming glow of green. Out of the corner of my eye, I catch glimpse of my silhouette passing by the large windows of every shop. My heels click against the sidewalk as I make my way farther away from where my heart just stopped.

I chuckle under my breath at how my night has unfolded. Bitchy to heartbroken. Bitchy because I'm heartbroken. And then slapped in the face by the image of the same person who caused my heartbreak. Thank you, karma, for reminding me you're the bigger bitch.

He looked good even though two weeks rarely offers a vast change. I smile at the memory of his eyes staring back at me and tuck my head, pulling my fallen purse strap back up my shoulder.

April: Heads up. Trenton just left.

April: PS Michael really likes you.

A faint smile tugs the sides of my lips as I read her texts, but only for a moment. I'm still on the same street as the deli and I swiftly pan my surroundings. A small park sits across the street and I cross, making my way to it.

I take my time strolling through it. At this hour it isn't busy, except for a few couples scattered here and there, sitting on the benches, lost in their own conversations. The trees sway slightly as the breeze tickles their branches causing the soothing ruffling sound of the leaves.

I hail a cab when I get to the other side of the park and again, I'm grateful the cabbie isn't chatty. Matter of fact, after asking where I am going, he doesn't speak again. I can't imagine having to hold conversations with random people throughout the night. How many times would I lie straight through my teeth?

He pulls to the curb in front of my house and I pay him before climbing out and taking a deep breath of fresh air to rid my nose of the stinky tree hanging from his rearview mirror. I make my way to the porch and sit in the rocking chair in the dark enjoying the night sounds. Off in the distance, lightning lights up the clouds, flickering purple and blues into the blackness of the sky.

A push of colder air washes over me as the cold front carrying the storm begins to charge through and I descend into the warm, safe confides of the house. I smirk at the couch. I've wanted to be with it all night and I finally can, but first I'm getting out of these strangling clothes and into something more comfortable before it can take me on a date.

I pour a glass of red wine, turn on the television, and scroll through the movies. Lucas complains about my love for animations. He isn't here, so guess what I'm watching? Something cartoony to brighten my spirits.

Chapter 30

I'm awakened by a distinctive soft tap on my door...or at least I think so. I haven't been asleep for too long because the movie is still playing. I sit up and then hear it again. I stare at it in disbelief, knowing in my gut who it is.

Even when I feel it in my soul, I'm not prepared emotionally when I pull open the door and see Trenton with his hands in his pockets. Instantly, I want to throw myself into his arms. Weep into his neck and beg for forgiveness, but I restrain myself.

"Hi," I greet him tenderly, hiding my excitement. "What are you doing here?"

"I expected the next time I saw you you'd be with Brian." His voice strains and he clears his throat.

I press my lips together and shake my head. "No."

"I'm sorry to hear that."

I tilt my head displaying a lopsided grin. "No you're not."

He expels air through his nose. "You're right. You deserve better."

Resting my head on the corner of the door, I say. "I'm taking your advice. I'm looking ahead of me."

"That's good to hear. How's it working for you?"

Hopeless... "One step in front of the other."

His emotional and gentle eyes haven't left mine. He hasn't moved. This feels like closure, ending a gaping goodbye. And as melancholy resolves around us, cradling us in its woeful arms, a sense of acceptance grips my heart.

"I miss you." My courage makes a path. If this is goodbye, I want to say everything I need to and find a way to apologize. "You were right. You were the hardest thing I had to walk away from." My voice drowns in deep ruefulness. "Even though it wasn't my choice, the result was my fault. It took me losing you to realize how deeply I felt about you. And the only thing that was holding me back was a paralyzing fear of change. For that I'm sorry. I'm sorry I got you involved. It's not how I hoped things would've ended."

"And if it was up to you, how would things have ended?"

I smile brokenhearted. "It wouldn't have."

The muscles in his jaw tighten.

This is torture—standing here with him in arm's reach. Seeing him. Breathing him. I close my eyes, fighting back the tears threatening to make a presence. No other words. There's nothing left to say except to finalize it.

"Goodbye, Trenton."

Two words felt like my last breath.

Our gazes don't falter as I step back and begin to shut the door. He doesn't move. His doleful expression makes no movement.

"Wait." He stops the door from shutting all the way. "I swore I wouldn't come by here. I tried, but somehow I ended up in front of your house staring at it. I don't remember driving. Seeing you tonight..." He trails off and for the first time, I get a deeper glimpse of the emotions he's battling. "I'm missing a pretty important piece of the puzzle."

"Don't." I hold up a finger, giving up the fight with my tears. "Don't tell me things I want to hear."

"Everything that happened between us...I have one regret and it's never telling you. I protected myself instead of leading you to me. I relied on my actions, hoping and praying you saw it." His voice cracks and it shatters me into a sob. "I never fully revealed how immeasurable you are. I love you, Riley."

"You asshole," I weep into my hands. "You can't tell me that and then walk out. It's not fair." He wraps me in his arms and I try pushing him away. "You can't..."

"Tell me you want me to leave and I'll leave." His voice shakes with emotion.

I grip his shirt, burying my face into his chest.

"Tell me, Riley..." he breathes out.

Ugly tears seep into the fabric of his shirt. He cups my chin, bringing my face to his. I blink his image clear. "If you want me in your life to stay, prove to me I'm not just doing this to lay pain across my own heart. Prove to me you are the angel who owns my entire existence. Prove to me my feelings aren't in vain."

"I love you..." I breathe. "And I don't want to stop."

His lips crash into mine captivating me with the depth of passion behind it. With a sense of urgency to feel him, his hands, his love all over me, I become frantic, running my fingers into his hair, and I pull him deeper.

He flattens his hand on my back and pulls my body against his, backing us down the hallway. He tugs my shirt over my head, repeating the same with his and cups my breast while I dig my palms against the skin of his chest. He pushes me down on the bed, his hazel eyes swarming with a lascivious glare as he rips my pants down my legs and shoves out of his.

He crawls up my body, nestling in between my legs and wasting no time claiming what he wants. Shoving forward, he enters gradually, releasing a hiss and drops his head beside mine.

We rock together, our moans and grunts echoing off the walls.

"Tell me again," I moan, needing to hear it again.

He pushes to his elbows leveling his view with mine. "I love you, Angel." He propels forward. "I fucking love you." He shoves again. "I don't want to ever lose you again."

He reclaims my mouth and pumps fiercely into me.

"Promise me, Angel," he groans. "Promise me it's you and me."

No words. I can't put anything together as my body ceases and I'm slammed by my orgasm. He burrows, giving me strong and long strokes, dragging in and out of me over and over as I thrash beneath him. He pulls every morsel of pleasure from me, lifting my leg over his shoulder and driving earnestly.

Watching me lose myself with a ravenous stare, a shudder racks his body. His nostrils flare and he clenches his teeth, surging into me, growling and pushing with force.

We both ride out our phenomenal waves. He drags himself out of me and drops to my side but doesn't make a move to touch me and stares at the ceiling trying to catch his breath.

I curl against him and he wraps one arm around my shoulder as I draw random lines over the bare skin of his torso.

"Tell me this is real," he says after catching his breath. "That I'm not wasting my time because, Angel, I swear I'm done begging for you. I'm done hurting."

I push up to my elbow and drag the backs of my fingers along his cheek and smile tenderly. "Claim me, Trenton. I'm yours."

Epilogue

Everyone has a road they're supposed to travel. Sometimes it's a clear path without any debris atop the bright golden bricks leading the way. Other times, the bricks lose their polished shine and the world around is dark with a thick murky fog making it nearly impossible to find the way.

I learned the past is the past for a reason and if you don't ever leave it alone, you'll never know what the future holds. Even though it lays a foundation for your future, changing one thing will cause it to collapse and you'll be left sifting through the rubble wondering how to rebuild it. If you learn from your experiences and accept the value of each lesson from each experience, you'll grow, hopefully bettering yourself.

All my roads were bumpy, rutted out because of my own self-doubts but I don't regret any of my decisions. I had to go through them all to understand and realize where my heart was taking me. My only regret was I didn't listen to the one thing that's never guided me astray—my gut. I was too caught up in the "what ifs" that I forgot the "what abouts" happening before me.

In the aftermath, once the air cleared from the ashy dust, I figured out Brian was only a chapter at the beginning of my story. He was an essential piece of my puzzle because without him, I wouldn't have Lucas, and without Lucas, I wouldn't be here.

I stood on Trenton's door step and declared my feelings for him in a desperate urgency, but failed to say the three words I knew I should've. It wasn't in a loving setting you marvel over for the next sixty years only to brag to your grandkids about. No. I lost that moment because of my past. I lost the euphoria of having a romantic evening and hearing the three most anticipated words in a relationship. Instead, they were exchanged out of despair, anger, and hurt. Not a grand story to boast about in later years.

But I gained more than I lost and I'll forever hold that close to me. I gained a future when I finally decided to let go of the past. I nabbed the one I'm supposed to be with, the one I know I'm meant for. The same man who shifted the earth out from under my feet without even speaking to me.

I get to witness daily what love is...what true love consists of. Every day our lives are passionate, affectionate, and engrossed with love. Even with disagreements, there isn't any disrespect. Instead, we spat and then figure a way to compromise or work past it—together. I don't live my life isolated, excluded from the world out of loneliness. I can't tell you what being unloved feels like anymore.

The baby starts crying and I groan, flopping my hand on Trenton's chest. "Whose night is it?"

He clutches my hand and squeezes. "If I said yours, how long would I get away with it?"

"There's a possibility I'd drop your coffee on the floor when I hand it to you," I snort.

He chuckles sitting up. "You're not playing fair."

I cuddle into my pillow. "I learned from the best."

He slaps my ass and when I jerk around to smack him back, he's already across the room opening the door. "Slow poke," he whispers, shutting it behind him.

"Shhh..." I hear him through the monitor. "We can't be waking up brother."

Ellie coos as the rustling sounds of him picking her up cause the green lights on the monitor to flicker back and forth.

"You'll make Mommy and Daddy so happy when you start sleeping through the night."

I can't help but laugh.

When we started over, we got serious quickly. Not long after he asked me to move in with him. Of course, my answer was a prompt yes. I didn't need to think about it. Lucas jumped all over it too. I thought it would mess with his head, but I was dead wrong. He loves Trenton just as Trenton loves him.

We only had been dating a year when Trenton asked me to marry him. It was so sweet. We were in front of the park's fountain. Lucas was there. And Trenton was on his knee. I cried when I said yes. We married six months later in an intimate setting. I didn't want anything big. Lucas was Trenton's best man and of course, April was my matron of honor. We didn't have a large audience. It only consisted of four of Trenton's friends and a select few of his family members. Afterward, he surprised me with an unplanned honeymoon and flew me to the Dominican Republic.

We were married close to two years when Trenton brought up the subject of children. That was fifteen months ago. Ellie was born in the middle of the afternoon on a Wednesday after making sure I remained in labor for an ungodly amount of time. But once she made her grand entrance, it was already apparent she had her daddy's heart. That girl could make him walk on the interstate blindfolded.

Lucas was ecstatic he had a little sister...that was until reality hit him. It's funny to watch an almost sixteen-year-old gag and flee the room over poopy diapers.

Can you believe my first born, my baby boy gets his license next month? I couldn't be more proud of him. He plays for the high school's varsity soccer team and still brings home A's and B's.

As for Brian, we found a pretty even happy medium. We co-parent well and have learned we make a good team as friends. He's got a girlfriend he's serious about, and although I've told him many times he needs to marry her, he refuses it. Brooke *says* she's okay with it. Yeah. I've been there too. Trying over and over to convince yourself it's just fine, but in the end, there's a significant importance missing. A closing step—the final stage.

"Angel!" Trenton yells with a guttural horror.

I'm up in a flash, battering down the hallway with my heart in my ears. The scream wakes Lucas and he's hot on my trail. When we round the corner into the living room, Trenton is pale, holding his hands out with a disgusted face. "She shit on me!" he shouts. "If that wasn't enough, she christened me with pee!"

Lucas howls in laughter and we both double over. I'm gasping for air when I rush to help him. His straight face does nothing to hide the humor in his eyes. This one is definitely going in the books.

Be the one to make you happy. Additions are always great, but ultimately, you are in control. Seek it. Find it. Cherish it.

And hold on tight.

The End

More From TC Matson

The Fighter Series

Blindsided (The Fighter Series #1)

UnExpected (The Fighter Series #2)

This is a continuance from book 1

Awakened (The Fighter Series #3)

This is a standalone and not a continuance from previous books

Acknowledgments

I want to send out a special thank you to my husband and kids for putting up with my drive to write and my absence. I love you to the stop sign and back. <3

Teabag-I love you hard, my soul sister.

Jessica-Thank you for our daily laughs, your amazing teasers, and your constant love for my writing.

Fran-You have brightened my life since coming in. Thank you for our brainstorming parties, your support, and your "you get me" moments.

Angela-Your support is incredible and your drive to see me rise to the top inspires me to do just that. Thank you for being the most remarkable PA anyone could ever ask for. You are my pillar.

To my Bangers: You keep me entertained, distracted, and lifted while, in your own special way, motivating me to push forward. You all have a very special place in my heart.

To the fantabulous bloggers: You kick ass! Point blank and period. You are rock stars. You are superheroes. And you're simply fantastic. Thank you for all you do for authors and readers. Your hard work never goes unnoticed.

To my readers: Without you, I am nothing. Thank you for giving my stories a chance. I'm honored to have my stories in your hands and ecstatic to see how much you've enjoyed them. I'm grateful for your continued love and support. And I promise to continue to deliver the stories that keep you falling in love with my characters.

Special thanks to:

Anne Mercier and Harper Bentley for always guiding me the right way
and encouraging me to keep on keeping on. :)

About the Author

"Dreaming in Reality...You dream in reality when you pick up a book and get lost in it. In my writing, I strive to take you to a place where reality and fantasy become a blurry line. Everything should be relatable. It could happen...couldn't it?" ~ TC Matson

TC Matson loves to let her character's voices be heard. With a head full of stories, she puts her keyboard through a beating daily. Matson sets her sights on writing stores relatable and real. And having an understanding that love isn't always instant and full of flowers—her writing mirrors it. She isn't afraid to push the envelope and touch the bases of uncomfortable situations.

She's a romance junkie at heart and an avid reader. Add those two together and she will devour books within hours, getting lost in the world the author creates.

Matson resides in the peaceful Piedmont area of NC with her husband and three boys, where staying hopped up on caffeine is the key to her sanity. Chaos is indefinite and a sense of humor is an absolute must.

Connect with TC Matson

authortcmatson@gmail.com
www.tcmatson.com
Facebook
Twitter
Instagram
Book Bub
Amazon

Made in the USA
Columbia, SC
07 July 2018